Praise for *Shoko's Smile*

"Choi Eunyoung's biggest merit as a writer is that whatever she studies, she turns it into an extraordinary story."

—Kim Yeonsu, author of *Whoever You Are, No Matter How Lonely*

"This collection signals the rise of a talented writer. . . . We often grow close or distant to people without understanding why, but Choi Eunyoung captures what happens in our minds with her distinctly subtle style."

—Kim Young-ha, author of *Your Republic Is Calling You*

PENGUIN BOOKS

SHOKO'S SMILE

Choi Eunyoung is a South Korean writer acclaimed for her nuanced yet poignant stories about women, queers, victims of state violence, and other marginalized voices. She is the author of the bestselling story collections *Shoko's Smile* and *Someone Who Can't Hurt Me*, which have sold over 200,000 copies and 150,000 copies, respectively, in Korea and are being translated into several languages. Since her literary debut in 2013, she has received numerous accolades, including the Munhakdongne Young Author Award (2014, 2017, 2020), Heo Kyun Literary Award, Lee Haejo Literary Award, and Hankook Ilbo Literary Award. Both of her story collections were selected as the best fiction title of the year by fifty Korean writers (2016, 2018). She has also published a Korean–English bilingual edition of her novella *The Summer* and has contributed to many anthologies.

Sung Ryu is a Korean–English translator who grew up in South Korea, the United States, and Canada, her most recent home being Singapore. Her translations include *Tower* by Bae Myung-hoon (2021), *I'm Waiting for You: And Other Stories* by Kim Bo-Young (co-translated with Sophie Bowman, 2021), and the Korean edition of *Grandma Moses: My Life's History* by Anna Mary Robertson Moses (2017). She translated the Jeju myth "Segyeong Bonpuri" (Origins of the Harvest Deities) for her MA thesis.

Shoko's Smile

Stories

Choi Eunyoung

Translated by Sung Ryu

PENGUIN BOOKS

PENGUIN BOOKS
An imprint of Penguin Random House LLC
penguinrandomhouse.com

The story "Shoko's Smile" was originally published in *Korean
Literature Now*, vol. 42, on December 11, 2018.

Originally published in Korean as *Shokoui miso* (쇼코의 미소)
by Munhakdongne Publishing Corporation, Paju-si.

The publication/translation of this book was supported by the
Literature Translation Institute of Korea.

LIBRARY OF CONGRESS CATALOGING-IN-PUBLICATION DATA
Names: Ch'oe, Ŭn-yŏng, 1984–author. | Ryu, Sung, translator.
Title: Shoko's smile : stories / Choi Eunyoung; translated by Sung Ryu.
Other titles: Syok'o ŭi miso. English
Description: New York : Penguin Books, [2021]
Identifiers: LCCN 2020054881 (print) | LCCN 2020054882 (ebook) |
ISBN 9780143135265 (paperback) | ISBN 9780525506935 (ebook)
Subjects: LCSH: Ch'oe, Ŭn-yŏng, 1984––Translations into English. |
LCGFT: Short stories.
Classification: LCC PL994.18.U572 S9613 2021 (print) |
LCC PL994.18.U572 (ebook) | DDC 895.73/5—dc23
LC record available at https://lccn.loc.gov/2020054881
LC ebook record available at https://lccn.loc.gov/2020054882

Printed in the United States of America
ScoutAutomatedPrintCode

Set in Adobe Jenson Pro Regular
Designed by Alexis Farabaugh

Contents

Shoko's Smile

Shoko's Smile

I dig my hands into the cold sand and gaze at the black, shimmering sea.

It feels like the edge of the universe.

Shoko once told me that standing on the shore made her feel like she was standing on the outskirts of the world. As if she'd been pushed away from the center, away from people, until she reached the edge of the sea that was itself pushed away from the great ocean. She said it wasn't especially pleasant for two loners to come together, only to dip their toes in the water.

"Someday I'm going to leave the shore, and live in a city surrounded by buildings."

Shoko always said "someday." She said it at seventeen, and again at twenty-three.

She said she would someday move out to the city, someday travel Korea for a week, someday have a live-in boyfriend, someday quit her job at the hospital, someday get a pet cat, she would be up for anything.

Shoko's English was easy to understand. Although anyone could hear her distinct Japanese accent, her pronunciation was accurate and her consonants and vowels linked smoothly. Under a wisteria tree where a group of Korean and Japanese students sat huddled, Shoko said in fluent English:

"Someday I'm going to get a caterpillar tattoo around my nipple."

All the girls blushed except me—I laughed.

Shoko and three other girls were touring my school for a program called "Cultural Exchange between Korean and Japanese Students." That was the year the ban on Japanese cultural imports was lifted. Shoko was from a Japanese city I'll call A, and went to a small all-girls high school that was apparently a sister school to mine. She was among the four best English speakers in her first-year class, which was why she was chosen to visit my school.

The principal, excited by this small event, took the four students around to every classroom, in all three grade levels. The girls seemed inexhaustible, introducing themselves in cheery voices when they came to my class, their final stop. Shoko had a shy demeanor, but I suspected she wasn't actually shy and only spoke shyly out of habit.

In the days leading up to Shoko's arrival, Mom, Grandpa, and I cleaned the house whenever we had time. Shoko was in the same year as me, and I was one of the few tenth-graders who could speak English, broken as it was. This was the excuse my homeroom teacher used to ask Mom if Shoko could stay at my house for her week in Korea. Shoko and I remained about a handspan apart while we awkwardly made our way home.

I still remember how Mom's and Grandpa's faces broke into smiles when they saw us come through the front door. How they knew nothing about Shoko yet still beamed at her in welcome, just because she was a guest who had traveled a great distance. Grandpa's and Mom's animated faces as they greeted Shoko looked strange and comical to me, given that my family normally had trouble showing affection to the point of being too embarrassed to smile at each other.

"You must be Shoko. It's great to have you here. Our place is a bit small, but I hope you won't find it too uncomfortable."

Mom chattered away in Korean as if Shoko understood her, while Grandpa translated for her into Japanese and kept on smiling.

Go get me my ashtray, bring me a glass of water, fetch hot water for my feet: giving orders while watching TV on the couch was all Grandpa did. He'd be sitting where he always sat when I came home from school and only spare a brief glance at me before turning back to the screen. But this very same Grandpa had switched off the TV and was asking Shoko all sorts of questions.

His voice sounded confident when he used Japanese. Even if he had learned it from harsh Japanese instructors, it was the only foreign language he could speak.

My family didn't talk much during meals. We would have the TV on, out of habit, and watch soap operas or the news while eating as quickly as possible. But as soon as Shoko turned up, Grandpa started jabbering away in Japanese and chuckled so often that I couldn't squeeze a word into the conversation. It was the first time I'd ever seen him talk or laugh so much.

Shoko knelt on the floor and very politely listened to Grandpa with a smile. Just as when I'd seen her bashful expression in class, I felt something was off about her smile. I sensed that she wasn't smiling because she was truly pleased, nor nodding because she really sympathized. The gestures were simply meant to make the other person feel comfortable.

Now and then Grandpa pointed at me and cackled in Shoko's presence. I asked her what he was on about, and she said he was telling her funny stories about me. Like the time I forgot to bring my backpack to school and had to come back home, or the time I peed my pants listening to a ghost story, stupid stuff like that. Grandpa had been furious with my accidents when they occurred, so I had no idea why he was recounting them as if they were fun memories we shared.

Shoko seemed to find it easier to communicate with Grandpa than with me. There were many things we couldn't talk about in English, but she and Grandpa could talk about pretty much anything in Japanese. Grandpa asked Shoko to call him "Mr. Kim." He said he wanted to be a friend, not old and boring like some school principal.

It was an evening in July shortly before summer break.

Shoko and I were chatting as we strolled along a nearby river. She said my family members were kind and funny. I didn't reply. My English was limited, but I wanted to show her that I liked her. I linked my arm with hers.

Shoko stopped in her tracks and looked at me, her face stiffening. She said formally in English, "I am heterosexual. I am not attracted to you sexually. Or to any other girls. I like boys."

A little taken aback, I told her I wasn't attracted to her, either, and explained that linking arms was a common way to display affection between friends here, so she shouldn't take it the wrong way. She didn't quite believe me, but understood what I meant when she saw hordes of girls arm in arm at school the next day.

Shoko said she lived with her aunt and grandfather. That was why my family didn't feel like strangers to her; if anything, she felt at home. Her aunt was the real head of the family, but wasn't around much because her job involved frequent travel. Her grandfather treated her like a princess, convinced that she was the prettiest and smartest girl in the world.

"I'm his religion, his whole world. Every time I remember that I want to die."

She said that on rainy days, when her grandfather came out to meet her with an umbrella, she climbed over the fence into her house to avoid running into him. Once, when he used a portion of what little money he had to buy her new clothes, she chucked them in the trash can still wrapped. The thought of her grandfather seeing her as some kind of girlfriend turned her stomach. As soon as she was done with high school, she would take off to Tokyo and never set foot in her hometown again.

"Then I'll give you *my* grandpa. Mine thinks I'm the dumbest girl in the world and nags at me to lose weight every time he sees me. He's never bought me so much as a pack of gum, let alone clothes."

Shoko smiled quietly at me. It was a pleasant but cold smile. Like she was a grown-up dealing with a silly little kid.

The house teemed with a curious liveliness during our week with Shoko. Grandpa went to the grocery store to buy watermelon after Shoko mentioned she liked the fruit. Mom set a goal to learn a new language whether it was English or Japanese. We had trilingual conversations over a plate of rice balls made by Shoko.

"Say cheese!"

Shoko loaded film into her Pentax camera and snapped the three of us munching watermelon. And like paparazzi, she took pictures of Mom cooking dinner and Grandpa cleaning the living room. While Mom and Grandpa were startled, they didn't seem to mind the attention and laughed it off.

I barely recognized this smiling, twinkly-eyed Mom and chatty Grandpa. I might've easily believed them to be good adults if they were strangers I met on the street. Mom and Grandpa had always been lethargic and socially awkward. I used to think they were like grandfather clocks that had stopped ticking, that gathered dust and faded in color each year. Like people who had neither a goal nor the will to change, whose lives had come to a grinding halt.

It seemed to me that the strangest of strangers was family. Perhaps Shoko knew more about my grandfather than I did.

Shoko and I would rent movies on our way home from school. Most of them were rated R, but I could rent them without arousing suspicion if Shoko accompanied me to the VHS store. They were movies like *Great Expectations* starring Ethan Hawke as a painter; *Shakespeare in Love*, which had some racy love scenes; the Japanese horror film *The Ring*; and *Notting Hill* with Julia Roberts. We watched them in the living room with the lights off, sipping green tea. Whenever a racy scene came on, silence stretched between Grandpa, me, and Shoko.

"I've never met anyone who likes movies more than you do. Maybe you'll end up making movies yourself," Shoko said as I returned the VHS tapes. "Like a screenwriter or director."

Laughing, I shook my head, but oddly enough her words left a deep mark on me. Shoko's words held a certain power.

Shoko gave me a world map folded up in a square. She said the world was big and we were free to go anywhere. That I shouldn't limit myself to cities near my town, I might as well venture out to Seoul, Beijing, Paris, New York. I thought this was a funny thing to say, so I just laughed. No one in my family had ever lived in Seoul, and I assumed I'd also keep on living near the town where I was born.

I stuck the map on my bedroom wall and drew a red dot on my county and Shoko's home, City A. The two dots were barely a handspan apart. Then I marked cities around the world that Shoko wanted to visit. Beijing, Hanoi, Seattle, Christchurch, Dublin. I was awed by the thought of people living inside those tiny dots.

Shoko's first letter arrived a week after she left. She wrote that she would never forget her stay in Korea. And someday when she went to university, she'd come back and travel with me. She complained that Japan was too humid when she returned— entering her house felt like walking into her grave. She added that we should definitely link arms the next time we met.

I wasn't the only one to receive a letter from her. Shoko had written a letter in Japanese and addressed it in a separate envelope to Grandpa. The two of us sat side by side on the couch and read our English and Japanese letters. Grandpa kept her letter on the armrest and pored over her vertical writing several times a day.

Shoko was always fair with her letters. Grandpa and I received letters of the same length on the same day; on some days I was the one to find her letters in the mailbox, on others it was Grandpa. We practically competed to get to the mailbox first and sat together on the couch discussing the everyday goings-on in her life.

Shoko seemed to share only bright news in her letters to Grandpa. She ran in a race and came in first, she went to a delicious curry restaurant with her aunt, she went boating with her friends on a holiday, she went on a trip to Hokkaido. What she wrote to Grandpa were beautiful anecdotes that might belong on postcards.

Yet the letters I received contained only dark stories.

She stole her grandfather's money, but he pretended not to notice; she tossed that money down the drain; she sometimes wanted to slip poison into her grandfather's food; she discovered her aunt was squandering the child support money from her dad, so she tore up her aunt's underwear one by one and hurled them out into the street; she sometimes cut herself on the pelvic area with a sterilized knife.

At first her contradictory stories confused me. It was hard to tell which was real, what she told Grandpa or what she told me. But over time I supposed that both versions of her letters were true. Not every detail may have been fact, but all were truthful stories. No, even if everything were made up, they would still be truths. As her letters to Grandpa showed, she must've wanted to be recognized and loved, and as she wrote in her letters to me, she must've wanted revenge against the people closest to her, including herself.

Shoko wrote us around once every ten days. She didn't care

whether we wrote back or not. She continued to send us letters until she graduated from high school.

Shoko said she didn't have any close friends. There may have been people she appeared to hang out with, but she seemed like the type that didn't know how to build intimate friendships. That's why she never opened up to the people around her, choosing instead to write letters to foreigners she didn't need to meet in the flesh.

If I were Japanese and lived anywhere near her, Shoko would not have shown the slightest interest in me.

People say things like "Out of sight, out of mind" or "Love or even hate-love grows only when you meet often enough," but they didn't apply to Shoko. For her to call someone a friend, they had to be a safe distance away, out of sight and out of earshot, with absolutely zero chance of ever intruding on her life.

Shoko did well in school. She was positive she could get to Tokyo one way or another.

Her letters stopped coming in March, right after high school graduation.

In her last letter, she wrote:

Turns out I can't go to Tokyo. —Shoko

And to Grandpa, she wrote:

I wanted to visit you in Korea, Mr. Kim, but I'm not sure if I can now. I'm sorry. —Shoko

Grandpa held the one-line letter and sighed, saying nothing. For him, too, Shoko was a dear friend to talk to. He had even planned to take everyone on a trip to Jeju Island when she came to Korea after starting college. Once a man who bristled at any mention of Japan, Grandpa now said the country's nutty politicians were to blame and we shouldn't take it out on its good citizens.

To this day, I don't fully understand the friendship between Shoko and Grandpa.

Under the pretense of going for a walk, Grandpa continued to check the mailbox for Shoko's letters. Every time I phoned, his constant refrain before hanging up was "Shoko must be busy. Has she been in touch with you?" While I was sorry not to hear from Shoko I was too busy to worry about a friend's letters, having just started the somewhat bewildering and wondrous life of a college frosh. I was attending a private university in Seoul.

In those days I hardly thought of Shoko. I was dating for the first time in my life and preparing to study abroad. It was only when I began memorizing English TOEFL words that I recalled talking to Shoko in my lousy English by the river near my house. I remembered the feeling of her arm against mine, the look she gave me like I was a little kid as she smiled her courteous yet cold smile, her excellent linking of consonants and vowels.

All I knew was Shoko's address. I didn't have her email or home phone. I sent a few letters to her address but lost steam when I got no reply. Two years slipped by and I left for Canada on a student exchange program. I thought of her sometimes but not with much longing or loneliness. She was a big girl, wasn't she? She must be faring just fine. Maybe she was studying in a faraway country like I was.

When my studies abroad were coming to an end, I took an overnight bus and crossed the border to New York for a three-day trip. I was traveling on a shoestring, which involved surreptitiously packing my hostel's breakfast toast in a napkin and eating it for lunch and dinner.

On one of those days, I was sitting on the steps of the New York Public Library munching on my dinner—when I felt someone's eyes boring into me. I was being scrutinized by an Asian woman with a short bob. Not about to take this lying down, I stared right back at her. Slowly, she approached me and spoke.

"You're from Korea, right? Do you remember me? It's me, Hana. The Japanese girl who visited your school in Korea."

I nodded slowly. Hana was one of the students from Japan. Hana was one of the students from Japan whose face was unfamiliar but whose soft, low voice I recognized. Saying it was great to see me, Hana invited me to her apartment.

"I immigrated to America three years ago. It's lucky I got to visit Korea before I moved here. I remember my stay like it was yesterday. Everyone was good to us. I'd eat out with my host family every day. Whenever I ate stuff like grilled pork rinds or intestines, they'd all clap and cheer."

"That's nice."

"You were a host, too, weren't you? For Shoko."

Instead of replying, I nodded and stared at the edge of the table.

"Do you guys keep in touch? I thought she said you two were pen pals."

I told her about Shoko's last letter. About how she wrote a single line on not being able to go to Tokyo and then cut off all contact. That maybe I'd done something to offend her. That I was stupid, having never thought to exchange email addresses or phone numbers. With a faint smile Hana told me not to worry, Shoko was doing alright.

"Shoko went to a university in our provincial capital. She got into Waseda Law but didn't go."

It was Shoko's grandfather. He suffered kidney failure, which required him to visit the hospital at least once every three days for dialysis. Shoko's shopaholic aunt, who was nearing fifty, barely had any sense of filial responsibility.

What with her grandfather in that state, Shoko couldn't go to Tokyo. Hana said there may have been financial reasons, too. By choosing the school at the provincial capital, she got a four-year scholarship and a reasonable commute by bus. Hana added that Shoko was studying physical therapy and would be able to find a job anywhere she wanted once she graduated, that she had chosen the safe path.

I'd never really thought about the kind of work Shoko would

do. I'd just had the vague feeling that she was not someone to settle in one place. She used to say with breezy confidence that she could live anywhere in the world if she wanted. So the news that Shoko hadn't managed to take one step outside her hometown troubled me.

I saw in my mind's eye Shoko taking her grandfather to the hospital once every three days, throwing away her acceptance letter to Waseda University, keeping her travels perhaps to no longer than two days. The disappointment and curious guilt I'd felt toward Shoko vanished at Hana's apartment.

Hana went on about her life in America and her college. I tried to pay attention, but my mind kept wandering back to Shoko's situation.

Even so, why did she have to ice me out so abruptly? Or nurse her grandfather when she'd so desperately wanted to leave him? I didn't get it back then. I gave Hana my email address in case she came across someone who knew Shoko's email.

Hana never emailed. Maybe Shoko had asked Hana not to share her contact information with me.

In the summer of my senior year of college, I went looking for Shoko's house. I took an overnight bus from Tokyo and asked my way to her town. I unpacked my luggage at a small inn, where I meant to stay for at least a week. I figured that even if Shoko wasn't at home, she wouldn't be away for more than two days. *Let's just see how she's doing,* I told myself.

Only when I landed in Japan did my body understand why Shoko hated the country's humidity. The moisture in the air felt like sweat. As if sweat were airborne and gathering on my skin before trickling down, instead of coming out of my pores.

Shoko's house was in an alley that branched off a road next to the beach. It was a quiet alley lined with small houses. A pair of middle-aged men sat fishing on the dock. Hardly any young people were in sight, let alone children. The only sound came from the odd car or scooter driving by.

I walked to Shoko's address. The front gate was cobalt blue. No nameplate.

Now that I actually stood before the gate, I felt a courage I didn't have before. I was sure that at the very least, Shoko wouldn't turn me away. If I returned to Korea without getting to see her, that was fine, too. I think, at that moment, I was listing all the possibilities of my trip coming to nothing and trying to brace myself for each one.

The gate opened faster than I expected. A tall, white-haired old man was smiling at me. His swarthy skin had a reddish tinge. I tried to recall the conversational Japanese I'd learned in my first year of college from an elective course, but all I could stammer out were words like *Shoko . . . friend of Shoko . . . Korea . . . letter.*

Smiling, the old man said something in Japanese and beckoned me inside. I was greeted by a small garden planted with four-o'clock flowers and a glossy wooden deck. The old man gestured for me to sit on the deck. Taking off my shoes, I stepped onto it and sat down.

The old man sat a little way off and timidly continued to speak. I had no clue what he was saying, but most of his sentences contained the proper noun "Shoko." I remembered Shoko telling me that her grandfather thought she was the prettiest and smartest girl in the world, and how that suffocated her.

The old man brought me a glass of ice water.

"Shoko, Shoko."

His voice was tentative.

Then he said what I guessed meant something like *Soyu is here, Soyu from Korea is here*. Not the slightest noise came from the room. He tried turning the doorknob but motioned to me that the door was locked from the inside. Though it was a hot, humid day, I felt a sudden chill. Shoko did not want to see me anymore. All I was to Shoko was a virtual friend or diary, one she'd simply stopped writing in, so how dare this diary butt into her life?

The old man repeatedly assured me it was alright and, putting on his hat, gestured that he would step out for a bit. The moment he pushed through the front gate, Shoko's door slid open.

Shoko was wearing a sleeveless, yellow print dress, her long hair pulled up in a high ponytail.

She gazed impassively down at me as I sat on the deck sipping ice water. Then she trudged over and sat some distance away from me. She smelled of fabric softener. We sat in silence and just stared ahead. Shoko spoke slowly, still facing forward.

"I thought I'd be the one to visit you in Korea."

I said to the side of her face, "You're disappointed I beat you to it."

A pause, then Shoko opened her mouth ever so slightly to say, "I've missed you," the words coming out like a sigh.

As I was a little mad at her, I didn't tell her I had missed her, too. Yet hearing her say she'd missed me made me tear up.

Some lovers are like friends, while some friends are like lovers. Whenever I thought of Shoko, I was scared she would stop liking me.

But in fact, Shoko was nobody. My everyday life wouldn't change if I lost her right now. She wasn't an employer or a school friend I shared my day with, or even a friend who lived nearby. Shoko was not one of the simple cogs running the machine of my daily life. In all honesty,

Shoko was nothing.

At the same time, I hoped that I meant something to Shoko. The strange emptiness I'd felt since her letters stopped coming. The emotional vanity of not wanting to be forgotten by her.

Shoko's skin was so thin and pale that even the tiniest veins showed through. I asked if she didn't go out much, and she said she only left the house to take her grandfather to the hospital. When she did, she wore a wide-brimmed hat to avoid the sun.

I asked why she didn't go to Tokyo, whereupon she looked me straight in the eye and smiled, shaking her head. Then she went into her room and brought out a sketchbook. She flipped open the octavo sketchbook to reveal a series of simple crayon drawings. Some looked like slashes of color, some were tiny doodles in the corner of the page. I noticed sloppy letters scribbled in crayon below every picture. Shoko pointed at the letters and read them aloud first in Japanese, then in English:

"Half-burnt sole of a foot."

"Extinguished streetlight on a highway."

"Rotten, but only rotten, seed."

"Soldier marching out of step."

"Dictator with no zeal."

"Antonym of typical."

"But . . . typical."

"The strange echo of the phrase: I knew this would happen."

"Pigeons pecking the ground to their last frozen breath."

When Shoko finished presenting all her drawings and their titles, she pointed at herself and said:

"Me. Shoko."

Shoko seemed to have burned a fuse. Hiding my heavy heart, I lied and said she drew very well. Shoko said maybe she should become an artist, no, perhaps try her hand at writing? She gave me a polite, that ever so polite smile.

It was the same smile she'd given me as a teenager. Yet in that smile, which had struck me as so cold and mature when I was young, I detected a vulnerable and defensive attitude. I used to think she was stronger than me. But Shoko was weak.

She must have felt it, too. That I'd become mentally stronger, tougher than her. I was watching someone who'd had a piece of her mind shattered and found myself basking in an odd sense of superiority.

I told Shoko about my college life. About going to Canada as an exchange student, the occasional backpacking trips, the foreigners I'd befriended. I also told her about running into Hana in New York. Hana tells me you got accepted into Waseda University but didn't go. I heard it was because of your grandfather's dialysis treatment, I babbled on without thinking. Even as I talked I sensed I was crossing the line, and, flushed with that terrifying yet exhilarating feeling, I crossed many more lines.

"I didn't think you'd stay in your hometown all these years. Especially to look after your grandfather? It's not like you. I hear you need to take him to the hospital once every three days?

Dialysis is really tough, huh? Not just for the patient but for the caregiver, too. I had no idea you were so fond of your grandfather."

If Shoko had lashed out at me right then, or at least defended herself somehow, the things I said would not have come back to wound me so much.

Shoko smiled. "You're right. I'm a coward."

She closed the sketchbook and took it back to her room. She never showed me anything like that again. She came back to the deck and sat down.

"But the more you hate," Shoko added, "the harder it is to escape."

I was perched awkwardly on the edge of the deck. I tried to remember why I'd bothered to come all this way to meet Shoko. She was neither someone I knew nor someone I didn't know. She was too much of a stranger to call a friend. She hadn't been one or the other from the outset, but neither was she shallow enough to make pointless small talk to someone she hadn't seen in a while.

"But I'm glad you're here."

Pressing down on the deck for support, Shoko shifted closer to me. I didn't look at her, fixing my gaze instead on the four-o'clock flowers abloom in the yard. From the sound of her dress sweeping the deck, I sensed in Shoko a peculiar loneliness distinct to old people. I didn't have to see her face to know.

Shoko was ancient.

She hooked her arm around mine, her cold, smooth arm touching my hot, sweaty one. It made my hair stand on end. Shoko rested her head on my shoulder. I could feel the soft, thin wisps of her hair. She laced her fingers with mine and kicked her legs in the air like she was splashing around in water.

"Stay with me. Don't go back to Korea, let's live here together," she said brightly, as if the suggestion were perfectly feasible. I resolved never to see her again. It would've been better to remember Shoko only as the seventeen-year-old and bemoan losing touch with her, allowing myself to slowly forget her.

If I hadn't bumped into Hana in front of the New York Public Library, and consequently hadn't felt a mix of pity and curiosity toward Shoko, I could have erased her from my memory. I did not enjoy beholding the naked face of someone who could neither escape her pinned-down life nor manage to love it.

Just then, the gate opened and the old man came walking into the yard. His face was flushed even redder than it was before. When he found us glued to each other arm in arm, he stood rooted to the spot and looked away in embarrassment. He could have acted like he hadn't seen us and gone inside the house, but he just stood there. As if to say he would give us time to unlink our arms.

I tried to pull my arm free, but Shoko clung on to it with all her might. I jumped to my feet and shook her off as I would a rat stuck to my arm. I stood facing the old man in that small yard. A smile spread across his stiffened face, which was still turned away. But the smile couldn't conceal the tiny spasms rippling across his face. Neither of us moved, and we stood there for a moment.

"That man's obsessed with me."

Shoko wagged her finger at the old man and added quietly in English:

"Fucking creep."

Startled at what she said, I glanced over at the old man's face. He turned his head as if to hide the tears welling up in his eyes, pretending to survey the four-o'clock flowers. My eyes flitted back to Shoko. She sneered, looking amused at the old man's frail state. I thought of Grandpa back home. I felt as if Shoko had insulted my own grandfather.

"What did you just say?"

"I said he's a fucking creep. I wish he'd go off and die."

I was speechless. My body grew hot, but my head cleared. "I won't be seeing you anymore. Stop acting like a child."

Shoko laughed. "I don't even know you. Who are you?"

Leaning her head against the deck post, Shoko stared vacantly at me with her mouth slightly agape, like a dead fish. I recoiled at the sight and looked away. The old man, his frame slouched, continued to study the four-o'clock flowers as if nothing had happened. The pink plastic bag he carried held a few apples and juice boxes with straws.

I bowed my head and apologized to the old man's back, and left the house. I paid the extra fee to my airline and took the afternoon flight back to Korea the next day.

The plane flew low. It was a clear day. Glancing out the window, I saw the Korea Strait sparkling in the sunlight. Things looked flawlessly beautiful from afar.

I lied to Grandpa that I didn't get to see Shoko.

"I waited for days, but she didn't come home. Sorry."

Grandpa forced a smile and said, "All that trouble for nothin'. Ah well, think of your trip as an adventure. Let's forget about this Shoko girl. She was probably too busy. We oughta make allowances for that."

The Grandpa I knew as a child was a man who flew off the handle at everything. Even if someone's mistake was unavoidable, he would say that wasn't his problem. He insisted on picking fights instead of talking things out. He showed little sympathy or generosity and kept bringing up past grievances in fresh fits of temper.

We oughta make allowances for that, she must've had her reasons, let's forget about it. Such words were not in Grandpa's vocabulary. It seemed Grandpa wanted to avoid discussing Shoko altogether. As if he were trying to protect his feelings by believing Shoko must've had her reasons.

How could exchanging some damn letters mean so much to him? Pen-palling with a foreigner who was fifty years his junior, no less. Despite having no money or real job since turning fifty, Grandpa had never learned to bend his knee to anyone. Yet here he was, resigning himself to Shoko's silence. The drawer of the living room coffee table in which he kept all her letters was now empty. He no longer checked the mailbox. From that day on, we never mentioned Shoko again.

Sometimes the image of Shoko, a doll affixed to that small house, would flicker past my eyes like a ghost. I assumed she had become a physical therapist. She would be earning money, too. At the time, I thought that Shoko had made a rash decision. That choosing a career at only twenty-three and confining herself in her tiny hometown was a bad idea.

Those were the days when I believed my life would turn out special. I secretly sneered at cowards who compromised with reality. But this silly arrogance of mine is the reason why I am nothing now. Back then I imagined that my life would play out very differently from Shoko's materialistic and repressed one, that I'd enjoy a life in which every day was free and true.

After finishing my English literature degree, I signed up for film classes run by a TV network. I had to tutor English in the evenings to earn my tuition. Starting out humble but determined, I wrote screenplays for group projects, learned about cameras, and attended talks by B-list film directors. I knew I had a long and grueling road ahead but did not doubt I'd become a film director someday.

One by one, my old classmates from college went off to work for banks, airlines, and publishers. I judged them for chasing money and security instead of figuring out their true ambitions.

A life like theirs seemed pointless. What I only cared about at the time was meaning, and I comforted myself in thinking that by following my dream, I was living a meaningful life. But I was scared. The odds of becoming a film director and making a movie backed by investors seemed next to impossible.

After graduating I sent my work to an independent short film festival. My submission was rejected without any comments. I rallied and spent a year writing a screenplay for a contest, but that was rejected, too. The people I had studied film with slammed my screenplay for being trite and boring and unoriginal. They read aloud lines that I'd personally thought were quite original and ripped them apart. Looks like you need more training, you need to watch more movies, I was told year after year.

So how long have you been writing screenplays? I was about to turn thirty by the time I started hesitating when answering this question. I'd been writing for five years and worked on some small films as part of the crew, but I was more talented at going to after-parties for various movies and listening to or spreading gossip.

I had believed that writing would give me freedom, liberate me from myself, shatter the limits of the world I inhabited, but reality proved to be the opposite. I was always pressed for cash, struggled to land tutoring gigs or jobs at cram schools, and grew touchy about money.

My spending habits became drastically different from those of my friends who were already managers at their companies. They never let me get the bill. It was out of consideration, but every such moment dented my pride. Friends with stable office jobs spent their weekends watching movies or performances and still found the time to read, whereas the amount of reading I got done was embarrassingly small compared to theirs.

When I met with my filmmaker friends, on the other hand, I always compared their talent with mine and wallowed in feelings of inferiority. My inspiration ran dry and only my monstrous ego fattened with each day. Watching aspiring directors whose failures had turned them into alcoholics and the screenwriter hopefuls who worked alongside middle or high schoolers without even getting paid for overtime, I told myself that at least I was better than them.

So, my dream was a sin. No, it wasn't even a dream.

If filmmaking was my dream, if that was why I pursued it, at least some part of it would've made me feel rewarded and happy. But I was writing scripts and making movies I didn't care about, just to keep the promise I made to myself that I'd become a director. I deluded myself into hoping that my movies would stir another person's heart when I myself was unmoved by them.

My creative vision had died in me long ago. I just wanted to be someone important in the industry. I was writing, but my stories were contrived as they didn't flow from within me. I wrote not because I wanted to but because I had to.

Dreams. They were a mirage, blotched with ugly feelings like vanity, ambition, need for recognition, spite. People who told me in a drunken slur that they "couldn't live without film" or were "desperate to make movies" reeked of thwarted desires. My desires were just as strong, if not stronger, but I put on a performance of not being desperate.

Pure dreams were meant for talented filmmakers who could afford to enjoy their jobs. Glory was meant for them, too. Film, art in general, only revealed its true face to hardworking geniuses, not hardworking mediocrities. I covered my face with my hands and sobbed. It was difficult to accept that fact. The moment untalented people clutch at the mirage of dreams, it slowly eats away their lives.

I lost most of the people I'd called friends before I got into filmmaking. Some remained loyal yet they, too, were judged by my ego, which had amassed itself feeding on shadows. A friend who married a man with a high salary was obviously a gold digger; another friend who confided to me about her soul-sucking job made me gloat inside while I put on a sympathetic face. I was shocked by the nastiness of my own thoughts, but even that didn't last long.

I spent longer hours at home alone. Oftentimes I wanted to see no one, and didn't bother visiting or calling Mom and Grandpa. While distancing myself from the few people who loved me, I thought my films would portray some deep layer of the human psyche. Little did I know then how lonely this arrogance of mine made them feel.

Grandpa phoned around three o'clock. I was still in bed.

"Hello?"

"You still sleepin'? I'm in front of your house."

It was a rainy day in November. I hung up and saw on my mobile that I had five missed calls from Grandpa, the first one at eight in the morning. I had no idea how long he'd been waiting outside.

Grandpa's camel beret was soaking wet. His nose and ears were red.

"Sheesh, how many people live on one floor?"

Grandpa clucked his tongue at the closely spaced doors as he walked down the hallway. I entered my room and pulled up the desk chair for Grandpa.

"No need for a darn chair. I'm comfortable on the floor."

I sat down beside him, but he shouted that women shouldn't sit on cold floors and made me take the chair.

"Grandpa, you need to quiet down. The walls aren't very soundproof."

"Quiet down, my foot."

Grandpa had brought a box of vitamin drinks as if he were paying me a sickbed visit. I took out a bottle from the box and handed it to him.

"I don't need that stuff. You drink it. You're always on about how busy you are, so I came to see for myself. And I wondered how you were gettin' on. Well, this place ain't much to look at. How would a girl meet a man if these are all the clothes she's got?"

"If you're going to give me that crap, you can leave."

This was Grandpa's first visit to the room I was renting in Seoul. He belonged to the couch back home or the jade heating mat in his room. He sat awkwardly in my space. He had gotten on the train, taken the subway then the bus, and braved the rain to see me. This wasn't like him. He may tell you to visit, but he wasn't the kind of man to go out of his way to visit you.

I've written "This wasn't like him" or something to that effect several times here. But now I think that the Grandpa I knew was only a fraction of who he was. Timewise, three-fifths of his life is unknown to me.

Grandpa was, at the end of the day, just a guest passing through my room. This strange old man—the old man who had to stand helplessly in the rain on an unfamiliar street, a nobody in other people's eyes, who would be remembered as a failure of failures—sat across from me pretending to look around the room.

He was the one who'd raised me and carried me on his back while Mom went out to work. It was under his care that my flesh and bones grew and my blood flowed. I felt that I owed Grandpa a debt in spite of the people who said filial piety was just an ideology. I had done nothing for him, material or immaterial. Maybe that was why I strove harder to turn my back on him.

Grandpa delicately fished something out of his pocket and pressed it into my hand. It was an unopened envelope.

"It's from Shoko. She wrote to us again."

He retrieved another envelope from an inside pocket and

proudly showed me its contents: a small pamphlet, Polaroid photo, and letter. Two women and a man in white gowns were smiling on the sky-blue cover of the laminated pamphlet. The middle-aged woman in the center looked like she might be the president of the hospital and the man and woman on either side of her appeared to be in their twenties. That young woman was Shoko. The baby fat was gone from her cheeks; her hair and eyebrows were dyed brown. She'd applied so much blush on her cheeks that her entire face looked pink. Her eyes and mouth were stretched into an exaggerated smile.

In the Polaroid photo, Shoko was hugging a black cat with white paws. Its eyes closed, the cat had surrendered itself to her arms. Shoko was beaming with her teeth showing in this picture, too.

"Shoko's a physical therapist in her hometown now. At a very big hospital, she tells me. Says she'll give me a discount or somethin' if I come."

"You came all this way to tell me *that*? You could've just called."

"I just, I just wanted to drop by."

Silence fell again. Grandpa took out a cigarette from his pocket and lit it, fixing his gaze on the tip of the cigarette.

"Who smokes indoors these days? You'll get me thrown out if the landlord catches you."

Undeterred by my warning, Grandpa went on to smoke his second, then third cigarette. I was about to tell him off but thought better of it, pretending instead to examine Shoko's face on the pamphlet. I didn't know what to say, or what his silence meant.

"You know, I never told you this, but," Grandpa began.

I remained quiet.

"I didn't know you'd grow up to be such an admirable woman. You went off to Seoul for school, became a movie director. Struck out on your own without askin' us to support you. You don't give a hoot and live your life. That, to me, is real cool."

Grandpa stubbed out his cigarette against a coffee can and peered at me. His face was trying to hide pity. Being a man who'd had precious little practice in masking emotion, his feelings were written all over his face. He knew I was sinking into a pit. He must know my life was lauded by no one, that was why he was offering these words of comfort. I had nothing to say except to look at the pamphlet and remark, "Why did she put on makeup like some kabuki actor?"

"Well, I think it's pretty. She can do whatever she likes, whether she looks like a kabuki or Peking opera singer," Grandpa said, standing up.

"What? You're already leaving?"

"I just came to tell you that. I've no mind to take up your time when you're so busy."

Grandpa knew I wasn't busy at all. That was why he could turn up at my doorstep unannounced. He must have been sure I'd be at home at three in the afternoon. I failed to invite him to stay and followed him outside.

My double-folding umbrella, the only umbrella I had, would not unfold. Grandpa was an impatient man and was already striding far ahead of me. The umbrella should automatically unfold at the push of a button, but the button was stuck and the umbrella wouldn't open manually, either. Heavy raindrops came pouring down. I was angry at Grandpa for not bringing a single umbrella with him in this weather. There was a convenience store at the end of the alley, but I didn't have the money to buy him an umbrella.

Grandpa slowed down from his brisk walk and looked back, giving me a wave and a sheepish grin. I clutched my broken umbrella and sprinted toward him. Gulping back tears, determined not to cry in front of him, I handed him the umbrella.

"Don't need it. It ain't raining that hard. Hey, why're you crying?"

I snatched back the umbrella from him and fumbled to open it.

"Because—because this umbrella won't open. It was working fine before. Of course, now when I actually need it."

"Well, you're crying over nothin'. Here, gimme that."

With a little tinkering, Grandpa managed to open the stubborn umbrella. He chuckled and held it over me. I told him to take it, but he wouldn't listen. The rain fell harder and harder. I offered to accompany him to the bus stop at least, but he said he was fine, he would go by himself. As he spoke his eyes turned red. They seemed to say, Let me go so I can cry. I released his hand. Grandpa strode off without a backward glance.

That headstrong and impulsive, yet softhearted, strange man.

My strange grandpa. That mess of a man. I gripped the umbrella Grandpa had held over me, watching his back until he disappeared.

Dear Soyu,

How are you? You must have forgotten me, but here goes. Before you came to my house, I had heard from Hana that she met you in New York. I got your email address from her but failed to send you an email after writing and deleting so many drafts.

I will put it simply. I was ill back then. You can call it an excuse. But that is the truth so I am telling you now. There were symptoms from the time I first met you and I still wasn't myself right before my college entrance exam. I wrote to you about a lot of things around then. Some were exaggerated, but everything was true.

You asked why I didn't go to Tokyo. Yes: I wanted to go to Tokyo more than anything. I thought it would be easier to die there. Because at home, my grandfather and aunt took turns keeping an eye on me. To make sure I wouldn't try to kill myself or whatnot. Grandpa caught me once and I lived, when I was so close to death. He saved my life, but I hated him for it then.

He told me there were people in this world who longed to live but couldn't, why was I having such self-indulgent thoughts? Shouldn't I toughen up? Cue a lecture on the samurai spirit. I don't think anyone understood that depression was an illness requiring treatment. My condition worsened in the meantime.

Grandpa didn't stop me from going to Tokyo. It wasn't him that needed me—I needed him. I feared I would really end my life if I made it to Tokyo. Even when I tried to kill myself at home, deep down I must have believed that someone would save me. I was scared. That's why I stayed in my hometown. I was relying on my grandfather and aunt in every sense of the word.

Most of the time I was in a stupor, and on the rare occasions my head cleared, I felt like I was a fire that burned my mind for fuel. I was angry at everything in the world, including myself. When the anger subsided, my body and mind would crumble into ashes. I went through this process again and again. They say nineteen, twenty, twenty-one are beautiful years. All I remember about those years is wishing day after day to die.

I vaguely recall that time you came to my house. It was around when I began taking medication. I remember being glad to see you (if I were a dog I would've wet myself), showing you my sketchbook, linking arms, saying terrible things to you. I was in a daze after taking my pills and felt nothing when you pushed me away. Even as you rushed out the front gate it didn't occur to me to follow you. I thought you would yell "Surprise!" and come back. I slept for a long time on the deck and woke up to find the sun already set. It was only then I realized, with deep regret, what I did to you. I had lost you forever.

I don't expect you to forgive me. You can blame me for writing this letter solely for my peace of mind. It's true in a way. I hope I do feel a little more at peace now. I'll write from time to time.

Shoko

It was daybreak and still I couldn't sleep. I had spent the night on the desk chair gazing blankly out the window, watching the landscape turn from black to indigo, then to bright yellow. I was looking at middle and high schoolers carrying backpacks to school when Mom called. Her voice was low and hoarse.

"Was Grandpa down to see you yesterday?"

"Yeah."

"Young lady, are you out of your mind?"

I was silent.

"A man close to eighty traveled all the way to Seoul through the cold and rain. Did it ever occur to you to ask him to stay the night, or fix him a meal at least, instead of sending him back on an empty stomach?"

Mom paused, heaving for breath. I could hear Grandpa's voice in the background. "I insisted on leavin'! I went just so I could see her. Don't take it out on the girl, alright?"

"Was it so hard to do? What did you have to do that was so important, that you drove the old man out into the cold? Even for you, that was immature."

I couldn't say a thing and simply listened to her speak. From her unstable voice, I sensed that her rage wasn't targeted only at my poor behavior. She was ranting at me as much as she was protesting at Grandpa.

I think Grandpa was mortified of disease.

After all, he had never been good at accepting the fact of his aging. I guess he thought being a sick old man wasn't very fashionable. How dare a petty sickness try to manipulate and destroy him? But that was actually happening and he couldn't stand it. His sickness was not something he could fight with pure grit and stubbornness.

This was around the time I was whining about having writer's block at drinking parties with people known to shoot pretty good movies. When I was spending my days "writing" at my desk, or rather clicking on celebrity gossip news, Grandpa had already been an outpatient for two years, I would later learn. He was still receiving treatment the day he came to my apartment.

I used to answer his occasional calls distractedly or not answer at all. Grandpa was someone who was always there. Whatever happened, he would be there because that's just what he did. All I was interested in was improving my situation and settling down so I could hold my head up. Grandpa never made a fuss about his health; if anything, he boasted that he rarely caught a cold in his old age.

Mom told me everything over the phone the day Grandpa was discharged from the hospital. She asked me to set my work aside and come home at least on the weekdays to look after him. You know I've got to put food on the table, I'll pay you a fair price, she said. As if she was sure I wouldn't say yes if she didn't pay me. But I had come too far to blame my mother for not trusting me.

Grandpa was absently watching a baseball game from his couch. He saw me come in but didn't move a muscle other than giving me a faint smile. Skin and bones. He was wearing the camel beret he had worn to my apartment. The red faux leather of the couch was peeling in places the back of his head had touched, exposing the black lining underneath.

I sat next to Grandpa and watched a game I didn't even know the rules to. A batter with bulging thighs got ready to swing, stomping his feet and wiggling his hips.

"This is boring. I wanna watch something else."

"It's almost over. Let's just see how the game ends."

I seized the remote from his hand and started flicking through channels.

"Knock it off! Hand me the remote, I'll watch what I was watchin'."

"Have I ever had the remote? You've watched all you wanted till now."

Grandpa tried to grab the remote, but his hands didn't have the strength. Though his face was screwed up in effort, in the end he couldn't take the remote from me. I switched to a fashion channel and watched a makeup tutorial. It was called "Eye Makeup to Seduce My Man." Grandpa walked slowly over to the TV and yanked out the power cord.

"If we're not watchin' baseball then turn the damn thing off."

"Do you always need to have your way? How can you be so selfish? Everything's fine as long as *your* mind's at ease? How about the rest of us, huh?"

Grandpa sat back down on the couch, hanging his head.

"Why didn't you tell me earlier?"

"Hell. You're talkin' nonsense."

"You happy now? With this mess?"

Grandpa looked up at me. "I really thought I was gonna be okay."

I wanted to say something—anything. But I couldn't move my jaws. If I did I would break down in tears. I suddenly registered how gaunt Grandpa's face was. I had noticed his body growing thinner, his skin sallower, but thought them to be natural symptoms of aging. I had assumed he was simply aging a little faster. How could I have been so acutely aware of myself yet so clueless about Grandpa's condition?

Grandpa took off his beret and put it on his lap. His sparse, white hair was flattened by the hat. He pleaded defensively like a man breaking up with his lover. "I swear. If I knew how bad it'd get, I woulda told you sooner. To pop by more often."

Grandpa mustered a painful smile. "If I'd told you, would you have come more often?"

I hugged Grandpa's head tightly in lieu of an answer. The top of his head smelled of oily hair.

Grandpa stayed sixty-five more nights and passed away.

Never had I been more awake than I was during those sixty-five days.

As if by an unspoken rule the three of us slept together in the master bedroom. Grandpa by the wardrobe, Mom by the window, me between them. The stories we exchanged in the dark staring up at the ceiling. Things we couldn't say before. Things we used to think didn't need to be said but worked up the courage to say. As if we were getting to know each other for the first time. Or learning to speak for the first time.

In the beginning, our conversations were either between Grandpa and me or Mom and me.

"Where did you move Shoko's letters to, the ones in the coffee table drawer?"

"Oh, those? I threw 'em out."

"Why?"

"I was upset."

"Why do you like her so much, Gramps?"

"She's a pretty thing, ain't she? Smiles a lot, too."

"Dad never told *me* I was pretty. I was jealous," Mom butted in.

After a few days, Grandpa and Mom finally began talking to each other, with me in the middle.

"Hey, Dad? You've lived on your own for forty years, right?"

"Sure have."

"Why, Dad?"

". . . How 'bout you? You haven't dated one man since you lost Son-in-law Lee."

"God, you're clueless. I have. Many times."

"Well, don't just go on datin', move in together."

The undeniable fact that Grandpa was dying served as beneficial poison for the three of us. But poison was poison. Morphine injections grew more frequent, and Grandpa vomited up everything he ate or couldn't eat at all. Not even canned liquid foods.

I wanted to talk to Grandpa. Even if for just an hour or two, I wanted us to switch off the TV and look at each other's faces. All his life Grandpa had been a gruff man with never anything nice to say, but who would've guessed the reason to be simple embarrassment. I thought about how he began killing his own embarrassment only at the end of his life so he could tell me things. He was born in an era that scorned the expression of feelings, calling it unmanly. Despite such censorship, signs of love had at times slipped out of him.

Mom and I stayed by his side in his final moments. And for that reason alone, I mostly forgave Mom and our relationship improved considerably after the funeral, to the extent that we could carry on a normal conversation.

I hadn't forgiven my mother for a long time. She went back to work as soon as she had me, and seemed only too anxious to brush my dad's death under the rug as if it were some shameful rumor. Over the years I came to think that she robbed me of my chance to mourn my father. On rainy days, I brushed past parents who'd brought umbrellas and walked home through the rain, while on other days I had the house key around my neck and took the longest route back to a home I hated returning to. Mom locked her bedroom door when she slept. My indifferent mother never nagged me with even the most typical parenting phrases.

Perhaps three hours before Grandpa passed, Mom booked a funeral home and packed the toiletries she would use there over the next few days. I gripped her hand as Grandpa's breathing grew labored. Her hand was hard and cold, without a hint of moisture.

Mom phoned the hospital for an ambulance when Grandpa stopped breathing. Her voice shook a little, but that was it. I slumped over Grandpa's thin body and wept, but she stood a distance away and watched. She didn't cry, her eyes didn't even well up.

Even at the funeral home she snacked on peanuts and dried squid and things in between greeting guests, striking up everyday conversations with an easy smile. The whispers of people in the restroom. Did you see Soyu's mom? She's as hard as nails, that one. I feel sorry for the old man, shame his only child has no heart. If only he'd had a decent son, this wouldn't be such a depressing affair.

Anger flared up in me at the people who knew nothing about my mother, yet judged her by what was on the surface; it was a foreign feeling, not seeing her from their point of view. Mom was a person who repressed and repressed her grief until she no longer knew how to grieve. A person who lost a father that she had lived with her whole life yet couldn't even let loose a tear without fear, who didn't know how to weep and retch and wash away the pain, who suffered only through invisible symptoms like headaches and cold hands and feet.

On the bus to the cemetery, I clasped Mom's icy hands, but they would not warm up. She stared coldly at my swollen face. The whites of her eyes were so white they had an almost bluish tinge.

"I want to cry," Mom said with a tremulous smile. Strands of her hair that hadn't been tied up properly were slipping down here and there. I took out some bobby pins from my pocket and tucked the loose ends into place.

"You think I'm acting strange, too, don't you?"

I shook my head, then nodded. "Yup. You *are* weird."

I couldn't have told her that back when I hadn't let go of my long-standing resentment toward her. Mom laughed a little and fell asleep on my shoulder.

We went through Grandpa's clothes and donated four boxes of them to the nearest Beautiful Store. The holed socks and threadbare underwear, the greasy plastic comb, the sneakers with loose soles, the pair of leather shoes covered in white cracks, and the almost used-up bottle of cologne were thrown into a twenty-liter garbage bag. Mom hardly hesitated before tossing out Grandpa's scrapbook, which was filled with professional baseball news clippings from the eighties and nineties. She set aside the reading glasses he'd used for browsing the paper and his dentures to put into his niche at the columbarium. His favorite camel beret, his summer fedora, and thick, navy felt fedora she moved to my room.

She told me to choose three photographs to place in his niche. I chose one of Grandpa hugging me in a bright, sunlit room when I was a baby. Then I picked up another one of him standing a handspan apart from Mom at her middle school graduation. Their hands were crossed neatly in front of them as they stood before the camera, not even holding the ubiquitous bouquet of flowers.

But there was only one photo of Mom, Grandpa, and me together.

We were sitting awkwardly around a halved watermelon. Grandpa was in the middle, his tightly shut mouth creased into a flicker of a smile. I was holding a slice of watermelon in one hand and making a V sign with the other, smiling uncomfortably. Mom was gazing expressionlessly at the camera with a kitchen knife in her hand. The photo had been taken by Shoko.

Neither Mom nor Grandpa had liked being photographed. Mom said her face looked too stiff in pictures, Grandpa said what was the point of photographing an old man. Perhaps Mom's idea of her true image was her smiling self, and Grandpa's his younger self. Shoko had followed them around anyway to take their pictures and they'd had no choice but to let her.

Shoko had sent the pictures to Grandpa along with her letters. In one of them, Shoko and I were standing a little apart by the river. I had on thick-lensed glasses, as I hadn't started wearing contacts yet, next to a younger Shoko smiling sedately. Back then Shoko had seemed so much more grown-up than I was, but now the Shoko smiling in the picture just looked like a kid.

Shoko's pictures had been bound with a yellow rubber band and stored at the bottom of a shoe box. There was a picture of Mom in the living room handling chives over a newspaper, of Grandpa and me hanging the washing out on the balcony, of Grandpa and Mom sitting on the couch with stilted smiles. There was also a picture of Grandpa in his beret, seated on a riverside bench and posing with his badminton racket as if to zap a fly.

I asked Mom if Shoko knew about Grandpa's illness. She said she didn't know what Grandpa and Shoko wrote to each other. Shoko's letters were not found in Grandpa's estate, either. He seemed to have disposed of all records except his scrapbook and photos. And Shoko hadn't sent any letters during Grandpa's last days as far as I knew.

"Dad spent thirty years cooped up at home," Mom said as she touched the part of the couch worn down to the inner lining by the back of Grandpa's head. "Would you believe it? That's as long as you've lived."

Mom pointed at the rubber plant at the corner of the balcony.

"He wasn't too different from that flowerpot. That . . . suffocated me more than you can imagine."

At just ten years old, Grandpa started working as a salesclerk. He looked after his uncle's shop flicking away on an abacus when he was still young enough to be throwing tantrums at his parents. Since his uncle had no son, his grandfather had decided to have him learn the ropes of the business. Apart from the war years, Grandpa never missed a day of work until he turned fifty, when the business failed. He was forced, at fifty, to sell off the store. It was due to his own little mistake, according to what he confided to Mom.

Mom suspected that he had been taken in by a close friend.

For decades she asked him what had happened, but he never answered and simply avoided people.

"I have no memory of Dad when I was little. He only came home to sleep. He didn't spend time at home until the very last days of his business. He was never around when I needed him, but just when I was ready to move out, he wouldn't leave the house."

Mom said her in-laws came down on her hard for making their precious son support her father. Furious, they demanded why a perfectly healthy man wasn't going out to work. But my dad accepted Grandpa, saying that the old man had missed out on the education he was entitled to and the fun he deserved. Dad normally hated smokers, but when Grandpa smoked with the windows closed, or sat all day on the couch without lifting a finger, Dad said it was understandable.

Grandpa always spoke highly of my late father. He said taking around such a handsome son-in-law made him proud, that Dad was a born storyteller who cracked everyone up at the dinner table, that he was a kindly man who never forgot Mom's and Grandpa's birthdays and gave them a small present every time.

Mom lost that kindly husband four years into their marriage, which left her to live with a mulish old man and a sniveling baby daughter thereafter. I turned Grandpa's dentures in my hand as I said, "You know the day Grandpa came to my place in Seoul?"

"Yes."

"Guess what he told me."

"What?"

"He said the way I lived was cool. Doing what I wanted to do. Oddly enough, I could finally get over filmmaking from that day on."

"What do you mean 'get over'?"

"I'm going to end it, Mom."

She didn't ask why. We organized Grandpa's things mostly in silence. She asked if I planned to stay in Seoul or move back to my hometown. I told her that whether I lived in Seoul or my hometown, I would not live with her. I told her to be free, to bring a friend or boyfriend home and hang out, to not worry about making anyone's dinner and just be.

"Mom, you've been dying to be alone."

". . . Thank you."

She handed me a wad of cash wrapped in newspaper.

"This is all of your grandfather's legacy."

"Why are you . . ."

"Just take it. He wanted me to give it to you."

Mom put the money in my bag and told me to deposit it at the bank on my way back. Although she could have wired me the money, she said she wanted to show me the banknotes Grandpa had saved up, bill by bill. He must have saved for years, judging by the old banknotes stacked at the bottom.

As I left Mom's house, I put my hand in the mailbox out of habit. An envelope touched my fingertips. The yellow envelope had Japanese written on the sender line and English on the recipient line. It was addressed to Mr. Kim. I stole the letter, pocketed it, and opened it on the intercity bus. Shoko's small, pointed letters leapt off the page, none of it intelligible to me. It was a one-page letter, written vertically. I took a photo of the letter with my phone and sent it to a screenwriter I'll call R, who spoke good Japanese.

This is a letter my grandfather received. I want to know what it says.

R sent back an MMS message.

Dear Mr. Kim,

I went to visit my grandfather at the nursing home yesterday. Brilliant white magnolias were in bloom, even on the shady grounds west of the nursing home. Today a patient who got an operation for severe neck pains texted to tell me she can finally change clothes on her own. A sixteen-year-old girl with degenerative disc disease said to me, after completing her electrotherapy, "Must be nice not to be in pain." Although I had done nothing wrong to her, I was sorry and told her so.

Mr. Kim, you asked me not to write to you anymore. Because not having to wait for my letters would be easier.

Ever since I stopped writing to you, I keep thinking about
what I could be telling you. Then I felt sorry. Whenever I
laughed, talked, worked, or ate good food, I felt sorry.
Thank you for everything. Please stay healthy.

Shoko

I wrote a short reply to the address written on the envelope.

Dear Shoko,

Grandpa has passed away. He passed around 7 p.m. on
April 5. He had been ill for two years and his condition
suddenly worsened in the past two months. You're the last
friend he was in touch with. Grandpa was always fond of
you and hoped you would come see him at least once. He
must have believed your empty promises to visit Korea, to
definitely meet again. It's a hassle to send handwritten
letters like this now. Email or call me on Skype if you need
to contact me.

Soyu

I pressed the letters of my email address and Skype ID hard into
the paper and sent the note by express mail. Then back in my room
in Seoul, disturbed by no one, I cried for two days. I remembered

how several months ago, Grandpa had sat chain-smoking at the foot of that coatrack in that corner. The fact that I could no longer see him became clearer by the minute. Yet the clearer it became, the less it felt like fact.

I was thirty. All I had on my résumé was a bachelor of arts degree and a filmography of two shorts. I could read and speak English without too much difficulty, but I had neither the certificates and score reports to prove my proficiency, nor any internship experience. Thinking I would at least need English test scores to apply anywhere, I opened the TOEFL book I used to study in college. I reviewed grammar and memorized a hundred words every day. Then my mind cleared and I found it easy to focus, like when you knit. Focusing on simple memorization slowly dispelled unwelcome thoughts.

Back when I wrote screenplays, I would be laughing one day and crying the next. Writing came easily to me on a good day and I'd think I could actually pull this off, only to throw it away the next day, seized by the fear that I would never be able to write again. People said you had to write every day. I wrote every day for at least five years, without my writing becoming any better. My muscles were paralyzed with dread, the dread that I would create only meaningless scenes even if I wrote for the rest of my life.

It didn't take me long to accept that I was not creative, was even less proactive, and felt rather comfortable with rote learning. For some time, perhaps I found relief in the conventional education system I had once loathed. While I memorized English vocabulary, I didn't forget to scour employment websites every day to search for jobs.

I would open my eyes at daybreak to the thought that people were nothing. Even the hard ground we stood on was, after all, nothing more than broken boards floating on a moving mantle. Despite my two feet resting on such uncertainty, despite being capable of only that much, I had deluded myself into thinking I could plan my future.

It was one in the morning when Shoko called.

I had dozed off studying vocabulary on my blankets. The caller ID was "Teresa." I sat up and took the call.

"Hello?"

The radio was playing on the other end of the line. The caller didn't speak for some time.

"Talk, Shoko."

Shoko began in a small voice, "I'm sorry to hear about Mr. Kim." Her voice was hoarse as though she had a cold.

"I'm sorry I didn't keep my word. But I couldn't go."

"Why not?"

"Mr. Kim didn't want me to see him ill."

Her words took some time to sink in. It had never occurred to me that Shoko knew about Grandpa's condition.

"You knew Grandpa was sick?"

"Yes. You didn't know, did you, Soyu?"

No. I didn't. So everyone knew except me. Who was she to know? A lump rose in my throat.

"I'm sorry I lied to you. But my promise to Mr. Kim came first."

Shoko pressed on before I had the chance to reply. She said she would come visit me and Grandpa in Korea even though she was late. Fine, I said, but added that I couldn't see her in my current mood. Jealousy of her sharing a secret with Grandpa that I wasn't in on, resentment at her cutting contact with me all this time, repulsion toward her behavior in Japan, defensiveness about my lack of stability, all these feelings converged and hardened into a cold steeliness.

"I won't see you."

Shoko said this would be her last visit if it comes to that, and she had something to give me.

"Mr. Kim sent around two hundred letters to me. I think they would mean more to you and your family than to me. I really want to give them to you in person."

All I could do was nod because of the lump in my throat.

Shoko said she was staying at a guesthouse in Myeongdong. I called her to a coffee shop in my neighborhood. When I arrived at the coffee shop twenty minutes before our appointment I found her already sitting there. Similar to what I'd seen in the pamphlet, her long hair was dyed blond and her face heavily made up with false eyelashes. She was wearing a khaki-green trench coat of a sparkly material and white oxford shoes.

My negative feelings toward Shoko stopped me from smiling even out of politeness. I focused my gaze on her glittering nails painted pearly gold. Shoko said she ate kalguksu noodles in Myeongdong, dropped by a nail salon, and got a massage. She said Seoul was a completely different place from my home, County K.

"Whenever I thought of Korea, the peaceful quiet of County K came to mind, and the middle-aged women riding around on scooters, the tall plants popping up all over the riverbank, the mayflies."

Barely listening, I held out my hand to signal I wanted Grandpa's letters. Shoko took my hand in hers and wrapped her other hand around it, too. She looked at me, a gentle smile resting on her face, and said she was sorry for my loss. To my great surprise, I was comforted by the gesture and the expression.

I remembered the sense of superiority I had felt toward Shoko when I went to Japan. When I thought so assuredly, My life is better than yours. When I thought Shoko was pathetic to hole up in her house and go nowhere. The memory of feeling inexplicable shivers when Shoko leaned on me and linked arms like someone out of her mind. Of watching her ill grandfather while feeling relieved that mine was healthy.

I had failed to see the shadows in Shoko.

"Here." Shoko took out two plastic shopping bags. "These are Mr. Kim's letters."

I reached into one of the bags and pulled out a letter. The penmanship was terrible. Written vertically, the letter was a riotous mix of kanji, hiragana, katakana, and numbers. In a corner there was also a drawing of two smiling sparrows with round heads and pointy beaks, their wings spread out as if they were having a good stretch. Though a basic, sloppy sketch, the joy of the birds was palpable.

An ashtray, phone, and notepad always lay on Grandpa's coffee table beside the couch. The notepad was for taking notes during phone calls, but it was closer to Grandpa's doodle book. He would while away the time drawing shapes, faces, trees, animals, bizarre patterns. Then he would go on cleaning sprees and chuck all his sketches in the trash.

Noticing my gaze on the birds, Shoko said, "Mr. Kim wanted to be an artist."

I had never heard this piece of information before.

"He wanted to become an artist who travels around the country and draws. But when he was ten . . ."

"He started working at his uncle's shop."

"Right."

I pulled out another letter. This one had a drawing of a baby elephant and a mama elephant poking each other playfully with their long trunks.

"He understood my state exactly. Like a doctor who could treat patients without having to see them."

"Oh, yeah?"

I passed the letter I was holding to Shoko. She translated it for me into English line by line.

"I was walking along the riverbank today and saw a young man sleeping in the shade. He could be thirty or so. His chin looked like it hadn't been shaved for a while and was covered with sparse fuzz, as was the rest of his face. I stopped and squatted next to him, peering down at his face."

I could see Grandpa, ambling down the riverside to pass the time, so clearly that I could almost touch him. In the street or on the bus, he would always watch other people's faces. I would hiss at him to stop staring at people so much.

Shoko pushed a bundle of letters from another shopping bag toward me.

"These are letters from Mr. Kim when he was sick."

I picked one and opened it. Drawn on a corner of the page was a puppy sticking its tongue out and bounding forward, its big long ears flapping in the wind. Shoko held the letter and translated it.

"I ate octopus porridge today. It's one of my favorite dishes, but it looked like someone's vomit and smelled awful, so I just about managed to force it down. My daughter told me, 'Dad, you've got to eat no matter what,' like a stern mother. I ate for my daughter's sake, my daughter who shouted did I want to starve myself to death. I ate as I threw up."

Why had Grandpa never said a word about any of this to me?

I asked Shoko, "Did he write about me at all?"

Shoko stirred her iced Americano with a straw, smiling.

"He boasted you were a carbon copy of him. When we started exchanging letters again, you won't guess how proud he was of you. He also wrote about attending a film festival that screened your movie."

I couldn't invite Grandpa to the film festival. I didn't think it right to ask a man nearly in his eighties to make the trip to Seoul just for that, and I'd already given out every free ticket I received to the people in the film industry I wanted approval from. I didn't even ask Grandpa if he could come to the screening. It was only after he badgered me many times to show him the movie that I played him the file saved on my laptop. It was a fifteen-minute short about a girl who loses her home and lives in an abandoned, half-constructed apartment before turning into a rat.

The film obviously received scathing reviews. They said it wasn't sophisticated enough because it drew too clean a line between good and evil and was heavy-handed with its metaphors. Grandpa, on the other hand, didn't give any kind of verdict and asked me questions instead. He asked where I got such an idea, if I'd really met people who lost their homes, he even asked if a person could really turn into a rat, and from whose point of view the camera was filming the girl. I think I was trying my best to avoid such uncomfortable, painful conversations.

Grandpa was my only audience.

Shoko chewed on her straw before she spoke. "There's something I never told Mr. Kim."

I offered no comment.

"You know when I wrote him again, that was six months after my grandfather passed away. It must've taken six months to pull myself back together. Mr. Kim replied to my letter. He told me he was unwell and was receiving outpatient treatment. I couldn't bring myself to tell him my grandfather had passed."

I thought of Shoko's grandfather. The man who had not made one retort to Shoko's insults and stood deathly still gazing at the four-o'clock flowers, his face burning.

"So I just lied. I told him my grandfather's condition was improving, that the doctors who said there was no hope turned out to be wrong, and so on."

Shoko gathered up the letters scattered across the table as she talked. "Funny, huh?"

"Funny."

"Hey, Soyu?"

"Mm."

"We're on our own now."

With a shrug, Shoko smiled her polite smile.

After that meeting, Shoko stayed in my room for two days. Together, we watched my two shorts, which seem as clumsy as ever when I watch them now. Shoko ordered in Chinese food to save time cooking and translated all of Grandpa's letters for me. She read them out in an even tone and speed, paraphrasing the words for which she couldn't think of the English equivalent. We also went to a sauna close to my house. It was there that I saw the light green caterpillar tattooed near Shoko's brown nipple. She pointed at the caterpillar, laughing.

We went to Grandpa's columbarium together.

Shoko wore Grandpa's summer fedora, I his favorite beret. His niche housed the family photograph taken by Shoko and a picture of Grandpa sitting on the riverside bench. Shoko's gaze lingered on both pictures. She put her hands on the glass door of the niche and called, "Mr. Kim."

We both laughed without knowing why.

Shoko did not stop by Mom's house. Neither did she go to the riverbank nearby, nor my old school she had said she wanted to revisit.

"I'll go next time. That way I'll have a reason to come back."

I accompanied her to Gimpo Airport. We hugged for the first time on the departure floor. It was the kind of hug where you put your arms around each other's backs standing slightly apart.

I remember how Shoko looked as she went into the departure terminal. Her face as she held out the boarding pass and walked through the automatic glass doors. Right then she looked back at me with her polite smile. My heart, as it had when I saw Shoko's smile years ago, went cold.

Xin Chào,
Xin Chào

We returned to Germany in January 1995. We had lived in Berlin from '92 to '93 before moving back to Korea for a year. We arrived at a small city called Plauen, which just five years earlier had been part of East Germany. Deserted buildings, empty parks, men sitting around at streetcar stops reeking of alcohol . . . it was nothing like the Germany I remembered.

The day Mr. Hồ invited us over for dinner, Mom ironed and put on a lovely skirt suit she rarely wore and dabbed on extra bright makeup. She untied my high, bouncy ponytail and whipped together a smart French braid. She made me wear the black corduroy dress I only wore to weddings and changed my two-year-old sister into brand-new clothes. I hadn't seen Mom made up in a long time and to my young eyes she looked very pretty. She kept checking her reflection in building windows. This was our first invitation to someone's home since we'd arrived three months before, so I guessed Mom was feeling nervous in a good way.

"Xin chào." Mom said the memorized Vietnamese greeting when Mrs. Nguyễn opened the front door. I chimed in, "Xin chào," and Mrs. Nguyễn smiled in delighted surprise. She greeted us like we were old friends she hadn't seen in years. Mr. Hồ was in the kitchen. His ruddy cheeks and boyishly mischievous face instantly won me over. Mr. Hồ was Dad's coworker, and when he discovered I'd become classmates with his son, Thuỷ, he invited our whole family to his house.

The dinner Mr. Hồ made was simple, cozy fare. I'm not sure if you can call food "cozy," but there's no other word for it. Beef stew with tomatoes cooked over a slow fire, fragrant steamed rice, grilled prawns, sautéed vegetables, savory fried dumplings with half a lime squeezed over them.

Once we finished eating, the adults started drinking and I followed Thuỷ to his bookshelf.

"I've collected these since I was six." Thuỷ picked out some books for me from the shelf. They were all Snoopy comics.

"Wanna read over there?" said Thuỷ, motioning to the low sofa. The suede sofa was soft and comfortable. I stroked it with the back of my hand as I began to read. Snoopy, who sat shooting the breeze with Woodstock on the roof of his doghouse, reminded me of Thuỷ. That's what Thuỷ was like at school. Ever chipper, he got along with everyone. Tall kids, short kids, outgoing kids, even the shy kids all seemed to love Thuỷ.

"You look like this guy." Thuỷ pointed at Woodstock, giggling. He added, "The first time I saw you, I thought you were Woodstock." I wondered if he was suggesting I was small and ugly, but I couldn't be mad at someone laughing so sweetly without a trace of spite.

"I saw you last winter. At the weekend flea market," said Thuỷ.

"How do you know that was me?"

"And from across the park, too. That was your house, right?"

"Yeah, what about it?"

I turned back to the comic book. I was embarrassed he'd seen me peeking at him from my window. Maybe he also knew how secretly glad I was to discover he was in my class.

My memories of Germany are hazy now, like a scene through a misty window. Yet when I think about my first visit to Thuỷ's house, the emotions I felt then flood back. I remember the friendly welcome Thuỷ's family gave us, Mom's joy at their hospitality, the warm feeling that we were accepted unconditionally, the very air in which our two families gathered in the same space and ate together. I don't know how it was possible for so many hearts to bond in kindness. Now that I've become an adult who can barely connect with another person, my time in Germany almost feels surreal.

During our first summer in Plauen, the dry climate gave Mom a hard time. White skin flakes covered her arms and legs like snake scales, and she complained of waking several times at night to scratch herself.

"I went through the same thing when I moved here. Korea has humid summers, too, doesn't it? German weather's the complete opposite. No matter what I put on my skin, it's dry."

Mrs. Nguyễn gave Mom a homemade lotion, telling her that applying it every day after a shower would help with the itchiness. Thanks to Mrs. Nguyễn's lotion, Mom spent the rest of the summer in peace. Mrs. Nguyễn understood our worries before we mentioned them. She came to the rescue whenever we had to call the plumber or talk to the landlord. Above all, she was the only one there for Mom, who was trapped in the house all day wrestling with a two-year-old. She said Mom reminded her of raising Thuỷ on her own, that when you were isolated for a long time you sank into dark thoughts, that Mom should call her whenever she wanted to talk.

Our families gathered for dinner at least once a week. We would eat at Thuỷ's one week, then at my house the week after. When the days grew longer in early summer, we'd spend time together from late Saturday afternoon to the small hours of Sunday. We started with supper, then the adults played their card games and the kids did jigsaw puzzles or read comics. I didn't know it back then, but I realize now that neither of our families had any close friends apart from one another.

On days when they'd had a lot to drink, the adults would take turns singing. Mom sung in Korean, Mrs. Nguyễn and Mr. Hồ in Vietnamese. I remember the adults bursting into laughter when Mom tried, unsuccessfully, to sing along to the chorus of a song she didn't understand a word of.

"Your dad and I can't seem to communicate," Mom used to tell me. Mom and Dad acted as if the other were invisible. Even when they ate or watched television or went for a drive. They probably never knew how much that hurt me as a kid.

My parents, both German majors, met in college and dated for years. When I was young, I didn't understand how two people who competitively ignored each other's presence could have been madly in love once. Every night I prayed that they would someday look at one another when they talked, have a normal conversation without animosity, that they would never leave each other.

That was why I liked dinners with Thuỷ's family. When they were there, Mom and Dad sometimes made eye contact and laughed, or casually told stories about each other. Once I even saw Dad give Mom's shoulder a nudge on his way out to the balcony for a smoke. I recall the indulgent gaze with which Mom watched Dad swapping boozy banter. Such things were inconceivable when my family was alone. I had never seen, and would never again see, Mom laugh so much.

You were really pretty then, I once told Mom. She said she

didn't remember those days too well, but thanked me for saying that.

In high summer, even past ten p.m., a little sunlight would linger in the atmosphere as if it were still dusk. I liked watching the light fade slowly, a bluish glow engulfing the landscape before me. When I felt the evening breeze blow in through the living room window, heard voices and peals of laughter from the adults in the kitchen, or peered at the sleeping face of Thuỷ, who always dozed off around then with his mouth open, when the bluish glow drained of color and one by one the streetlights came on, it hit me that I might one day miss this moment.

Thuỷ and I used to go on errands together to buy milk or bread. On our way to the store, he would sprint down the street out of sight then come running back. I tried to chase after him the first few times but kept walking at my usual pace once I realized he'd eventually return. I watched him disappear and race back to me, cracking up at the look on his face. When our eyes met he'd throw back his head and run in his silliest pose.

On our way home, though, we walked on opposite sides of the road. We were scared we might be teased at school if we stuck too close to each other. "Woodstock!" That's what Thuỷ always called me when we were alone. I was delighted by the name the more I heard it. As I had changed schools frequently, no one else had bothered giving a nickname to someone just passing through.

We walked side by side only after we turned onto Thuỷ's street. When we did I caught a whiff of his sweat, which sometimes smelled like a coin baked in the sun, sometimes like onion. We didn't talk much, but simply walking together like that was comforting.

Thuỷ didn't have the waywardness typical of his age. He chattered about his day at school to Mrs. Nguyễn, and amused everyone by belting out a song or doing an impromptu skit with zero self-consciousness. I talked to him as though he were my baby brother, sometimes even sharing my deepest confidences in an offhand way. I did this on the assumption that whatever I said would be lost on a little kid like Thuỷ anyway. He didn't seem to care too much about what I told him. Yeah, yeah? Listening to his indifferent replies, the emotions I'd been holding in were let loose a little.

"My mom and dad hate each other the most," I said one day with a casual laugh. Thuỷ stopped in his tracks and looked at me, stock-still. He almost seemed angry. I didn't know what to say at his unexpected reaction.

"Why would you laugh when you say something like that?" Thuỷ said, then strode past me. I expected him to come back as usual, but he didn't. Though slightly taken aback, I thought nothing of it at the time. Yet later in my high school days, as I crossed the school field after study hall, I would sometimes recall Thuỷ's young face saying, "Why would you laugh when you say something like that?" I had known nothing about Thuỷ. It was only after my childhood that I began to remember him differently.

"When we first came to Germany," Mrs. Nguyễn said with a loud laugh, "it was really cold. I'd be shivering no matter how many layers I put on. I still do. Thuỷ was born here so he's fine, but I still can't get used to the winters somehow. The shock of seeing snow for the first time. It was so pretty that even as I complained about the cold, I touched and played with it until my hands froze."

Mom looked over at Mrs. Nguyễn's laughing face. I remember Mom's face being flustered because she was supposed to laugh along but she couldn't. Whenever Mrs. Nguyễn talked about tough times, she laughed exaggeratedly and Mom tried her best to laugh with her.

Mrs. Nguyễn said Mom had a big heart and the innate capacity to sympathize with other people. She said the world needed more perceptive people like her, that she was someone who ached for the people who couldn't ache.

She often complimented Mom when they were together, too. You have such a nice smile it lights up the whole room, your forehead is round and pretty, you have a graceful walk, you're a good dresser, you have cute front teeth, you have a pleasant voice . . . Mrs. Nguyễn would pay such compliments without reserve and make Mom blush. Listening to Mrs. Nguyễn, I noticed nice qualities of Mom that I hadn't seen before and was proud to call her my mother. Mrs. Nguyễn and Mom visited each other's houses almost every day. Mom roasted the seaweed she had brought from Korea and gave it to Mrs. Nguyễn, who liked laver seaweed, while Mrs. Nguyễn made rice pudding for Mom, who had a sweet tooth.

During my second winter in Plauen, I hung out at Thuỷ's nearly every day. My house was always chilly because the radiator was old, but Thuỷ's was so pleasantly warm that my whole body mellowed out when I was there. Besides, I felt more comfortable around Thuỷ's family than I did around mine.

Mrs. Nguyễn asked me lots of questions. What was my old school in Korea like, how did I like it in Berlin, had I ever been to the sea, what color was the sea in Korea, what was my favorite German food. Her questions were different from what other adults usually grilled me with, like was I a good student, why was I so short, what did I want to be when I grew up. Delighted at receiving such sincere attention, I yapped on and on in front of Mrs. Nguyễn until my cheeks grew red.

"Can you write out the Chinese characters of your name?" Mrs. Nguyễn asked. I wrote my name in Chinese and she smiled. "I knew it. We have the same last names." She wrote won 阮, the character for "the state of Ruǎn," and pronounced it as "Nguyễn." Mr. Hồ's name was written with the character ho 胡 for "unit of volume," and Thuỷ's with the character chwi 翠 for "green." "You look a lot like a childhood friend of mine. Her last name was Nguyễn, too. She lived in the same village as me." Mrs. Nguyễn smiled sadly. She had that expression whenever she talked about things she liked very much. She had it, too, when she looked at my baby sister, Dayeon, who had now turned three. The more I saw that expression the more it pained me; happiness for Mrs. Nguyễn seemed to be too adjacent to sadness.

Once, I asked her to show me pictures from her childhood. She shook her head. "I lost all of them. I wish I had at least one left." When I asked her why, she only patted my head. "It wasn't just the pictures I lost," she said softly. I didn't know what those words meant exactly, but the tremor in her heart as she said them reached me so clearly that it scared me.

The only inaccessible part of Thuỷ's house was the study. No one told me it was off-limits, but the door was always shut so I had never thought to go in.

One day, the door to the study was wide-open, and I was magnetically drawn into the room. My eyes fell on a small shrine right next to the door.

The shrine was set up on a wooden cupboard. At the foot of a structure roofed and pillared like a house, there stood five picture frames and a censer filled with sand and ashes. Each frame encased a black-and-white photograph of a person and the censer burned a few purple incense sticks, some to the bottom and some halfway. Beside the censer lay incense sticks wrapped in paper and a small matchbox. I had seen such censers before, but that was my first time seeing one fronting pictures of the dead. I was afraid to look directly at the pictures and turned away.

The five people in the photographs looked like a family. If I remember correctly there was only one elderly person, along with a girl around my age and a baby around Dayeon's age. Although I had only caught a glimpse, their faces haunted me, clinging to my back.

I wanted to know who they were, why they were enshrined in Thuỷ's house. I was curious why neither Mrs. Nguyễn nor Thuỷ had shown me the shrine, but a vague fear kept me from telling anyone about what I saw.

I heard Thuỷ say something unexpected in class when we were learning about World War II. It was at the start of the fall semester.

"Fortunately, World War II was the last war to bring about such a massive scale of killings." Thuỷ put up his hand and interrupted the teacher. "That's not true." Those were Thuỷ's first words.

"What's not true?"

"A lot of people in Vietnam were killed in war. My grandpa, grandma, my mom's sister, my dad's sister, my uncles, everybody. The soldiers came and just killed them. Even all the children. The whole village was gone. I heard my mom talk about it," said Thuỷ.

"Yes. Thuỷ's right. Not many of you will have heard about the Vietnam War. Thuỷ, would you like to tell us more?" The teacher was satisfied that Thuỷ was sharing his opinion, but Thuỷ seemed to have blurted out those things as a reflex. I knew because his face was reddening like he was about to cry. He started to speak but then shut his mouth and lowered his head.

"Go on, Thuỷ. We all need to know." Thuỷ shook his head. Everything about that situation felt unjust to me, though I couldn't make sense of that emotion at the time. Just then the class prefect, Inga, raised her hand.

"Vietnam is the only country that ever beat America at war. Sixty thousand American soldiers died and two million Vietnamese people who weren't soldiers died, too. I saw it on TV. And the Americans dropped bombs from airplanes and sprayed a chemical that kills trees." A proud smile rose on the prefect's face. I looked at Thuỷ's small ears, which were burning scarlet.

The teacher praised the prefect for her accurate answer and explained why the US joined the Vietnam War and how the war played out. She went on to conclude that it was a mistake for the American government to join, as nothing was gained from the war. That's not what Thuỷ wanted to say, and explaining it like that in front of Thuỷ is hurtful, I remember wanting to say, but somehow I couldn't open my mouth. Thuỷ was clearly in the classroom, but at that moment, I felt that he was being treated as if he weren't. I watched him from the back as he sat hunched over in his seat. You all have no idea what Thuỷ's feeling, I remember thinking, even feeling a faint anger toward the German kids.

That night we were gathered around the dinner table at Thuỷ's, eating Mr. Hồ's noodles and dumplings. I can't really remember how the conversation drifted in that direction.

I was a thirteen-year-old girl who wasn't pretty and wasn't particularly good at anything. Ever since my little sister was born when I was ten, I was told to stop acting like a child no matter what I did. Like many children who have no presence, I hungered for adult recognition.

So when the conversation turned to Japan's colonial rule, my heart skipped a beat at what the adults were saying. Finally, here was my chance to put in my two cents. Since I knew more than Thuỷ's family when it came to Korean history, if I showed off my knowledge my parents would be pretty proud of me.

"Korea never invaded any country." I said that and looked over at Mom and Dad to seek their approval. Dad pretended not to have heard me and didn't glance my way; Mom shot me a silencing look. Mr. Hồ changed the subject: "I hope the broth isn't too salty." I was miffed that everyone seemed to be ignoring me. "It's true. We never hurt anybody," I said. I wanted to give them the impression that Korea was a nice country, and also to casually join the adults' conversation and receive a compliment. I looked hopefully at Dad, who was sitting across from me.

"Don't butt in when the adults are speaking. Keep your mouth shut if you don't know what you're talking about!" Dad shouted in Korean. Everyone stopped using their chopsticks, their eyes on me now. Embarrassed and indignant at being told off by Dad like that in front of Thuỷ's family, my ears were ringing and my eyes welled up with tears. My face burned. I screwed up my last ounce of courage and said in German, "But that's how I was taught in Korea. That we never did anything wrong to anyone. That we've only ever been wronged. That's what my teacher said . . ."

"I heard it was the Korean soldiers who killed them," Thuỷ said. His voice was small, but it was enough to freeze the mood at the table. "The Koreans killed all of my mom's family. My grandma, even my aunt who was only a baby—they just killed everyone. I heard there's a hate monument in my mom's hometown." Thuỷ's accusatory tone seemed to say, How could you say that? But I didn't understand what he was saying at all.

"Thuỷ, watch what you say," Mrs. Nguyễn said, and turned to me. "Don't worry about it. This has nothing to do with you." Her words only confirmed that Thuỷ was right. "It's really nothing to worry about." Those eyes that worried for my childish heart getting injured, that face I would never forget. It was when I saw this face of Mrs. Nguyễn that the truth of Thuỷ's words sank in. If I were wounded at that moment, it would've been from the guilt I felt over Mrs. Nguyễn's wound. "It happened before you were even born," she whispered.

"I had no idea," said Mom. "I can't possibly fathom what you've been through, but I want to apologize. I'm so sorry." Mom bowed her head before Mr. Hồ and Mrs. Nguyễn.

"I saw everything with my own eyes. I was around Thuỷ's age," said Mr. Hồ, managing a smile with bloodshot eyes. "But thank you for saying that." Mr. Hồ stopped there and mustered a laugh as best he could. Mrs. Nguyễn murmured something in Vietnamese to Mr. Hồ. Though I didn't understand what she said, it must have been words of comfort. Because the vibrations of her words seemed to console my own heart.

Dad just sat drinking beer as if he hadn't heard Mom and Mr. Hồ's exchange.

"Say something," Mom told Dad in Korean.

"What's there to say? What, you want me to say it's our fault? Why are you taking it upon yourself to apologize? Who are you to do that?" Dad shot back in Korean.

"This is what you always do. You can't for the life of you say sorry—you *won't*. Is it really that hard? If I were Mrs. Nguyễn, I never would've given our family the time of day to begin with."

Dad took the cardigan slung over the dining chair and put one arm in. "Thank you for the dinner." He hesitated before he spoke again. "My older brother also died in that war. He was twenty-six. He was just a mercenary," said Dad, staring down at the floor as if he didn't want to meet anyone's eyes.

"They killed infants and old people," said Mrs. Nguyễn.

"It must've been impossible to tell the Việt Cộng from civilians in the confusion," said Dad, still avoiding Mrs. Nguyễn's eyes.

"Could they have mistaken an infant only a week old for a Việt Cộng? An immobile senior for a Việt Cộng?"

"It was a war."

"A war? It was nothing but a disgusting massacre," said Mrs. Nguyễn. Her tone was formal, devoid of emotion.

"So what do you expect me to say? I lost my brother, too, you know. Isn't this business long over? Would you rather have us apologizing over and over again for it?"

"Have you lost your mind?" Mom said to Dad.

Mrs. Nguyễn got up and slowly walked into the study. The careful click of the shutting door. I was scared out of my wits, but I couldn't follow her into the study. Mom took my sister into her arms and stood up. "I am so sorry." She bowed her head to Mr. Hồ. "I'm sorry, Thuỷ," she said, and left. I grabbed the diaper bag and cardigan and trailed after her.

It was nothing but a disgusting massacre. Mrs. Nguyễn's unsmiling face uttering those words floated above my own face as I lay down to sleep. When she said those words, she was in a different space from the one we were in. She was forced out to a place and time that I couldn't possibly imagine even if I tried. She wasn't trying to convince Dad, nor was she trying to defend herself. Those words were not even directed at Dad; I think they were a kind of bitter smile she gave herself, for struggling through all these years after what happened. She wasn't even disappointed with Dad's attitude. You lot would never understand anyway: this frame of mind had, on that night, safely driven a wedge between Mrs. Nguyễn and my family. It was a conventional choice made by adults who did not wish to hate each other, or be wounded by each other any further.

Mom did her best to repair our relationship with Thuỷ's family. Even I, a thirteen-year-old, instinctively knew that things couldn't go back to the way they were, but Mom didn't think so. Time after time she went to see Mrs. Nguyễn, taking me and my sister with her. Nothing had changed on the surface. Mrs. Nguyễn brought out tea and snacks and we chatted about this and that like before. But I couldn't help feeling that she was merely enduring that stretch of time. Mom talked more than usual as if to fight off the awkwardness. In such moments, her imperfect German often splintered to pieces and her agitated sentences failed to create meaning. Words failing to link up with other words drifted aimlessly about, sentences with mismatched tenses, genders, and numbers sounding like a contrived joke. Mrs. Nguyễn looked tired listening to Mom talk. Even if she was trying to hide her emotions, the look on her face could hardly escape our notice.

By the time we started wearing winter coats, Mom stopped visiting Mrs. Nguyễn and made no further mention of her. Saturday nights, which we had always spent with Thuỷ's family, turned into awkward television-watching time among ourselves. Since the days were shorter around then, it became pitch-dark everywhere by six and I was sent to my room by eight. Sleep didn't come easily on those nights. I lay still, listening to the sound of my mom dragging a dining chair, or the sound of her calling someone in Korea in a hushed voice. Once, I went out to use the bathroom at dawn and saw her sitting on a dining chair, staring blankly at the wall. I saw the pensive expression she had, unaware of my entrance, her surprise when she noticed me, her attempt at a reassuring smile as her eyelids trembled.

Mom threw her half-used lipstick and foundation into the trash, and tossed her favorite skirt suit and dress into a collection bin. Her Sunday ritual used to be packing up and venturing to the nearby forest, to the flea market, or the flower market, but now all she did was lie in my sister's room and stare at the wall. Even in situations where she would've normally picked fights with Dad about something he said or did, or hurled retorts at him, she stayed silent. She ate infrequent, big meals and knitted till her fingertips turned red.

On one of those days, I rummaged through the trash can in my sister's room while Mom was deeply asleep. I found torn-up pictures cast into the can. A picture of Mom hugging me when I was still a baby next to a smiling Dad, a picture of me touching her belly when she was almost due . . . pictures torn up into such tiny pieces they could not be taped back together. I looked quietly into the face of my mother, who was sleeping beside Dayeon. I feared she might be too far away, that she might slip further away.

Mom handed me a square gift box. Explaining it was a gift for Thuỷ's family, she asked me to deliver the box to Thuỷ. I placed the box on the kitchen windowsill. It was wrapped in green and yellow packaging paper with a red ribbon on top.

We were living like squatters since the few pieces of furniture we had were sent out and most of our belongings shipped off. We spread out newspaper on the floor to eat sandwiches and crawled into sleeping bags at night. As I had grown a lot taller in the past two years, all the clothes I'd worn in Germany were thrown into the collection bin. I didn't want to stay in Germany, but I didn't want to go back to Korea, either. I was due to enter a Korean middle school in a month. I had trouble picturing myself in a bob cropped three centimeters below the ears or standing uniformed in rows on the school field for morning assembly. Though this was certainly a scary change, what I felt then was not so much fear as resignation.

It was snowing heavily that day. As fresh snow was piling up in the park before the existing snow had time to melt and freeze, only a narrow side path had been cleared for people to cross. I sat on a large suitcase stuffed with clothes, looking out the window. The first time I saw Thuỷ was through this window, too. In my mind's eye I saw Thuỷ zigzagging friskily down the street, and my nose stung. The sun was about to set and the snow covering the park acquired a bluish tinge.

Just then, I saw out my window a boy with long bangs in a black parka. He was planting each foot forward in long strides. Although I couldn't see his face properly, I knew there would be a monkeyish grin on it. The boy turned toward the window and looked up at me, then he stretched out his arm and waved. It was Thuỷ. Picking up the gift box Mom had given me, I went downstairs and crossed the street.

There were only footsteps left on the spot where Thuỷ had just been. I stood there looking around, I don't know for how long. Then Thuỷ appeared in the distance, scampering toward me. He stopped right in front of my nose and burst out laughing.

"What's with that face? Seriously, how do you still fall for this?" said Thuỷ.

"Don't you dare pull that prank on me again," I should've said, and laughed, but I couldn't bring myself to laugh. It had just hit me that the word "again" was now pointless. I felt a lump in my throat.

"Hey. What's the matter, I've pulled that one on you a gazillion times. Alright. I won't do it again."

Thuỷ seemed taken aback to see me blinking back tears and surveyed me for a long moment.

"Are you a sled dog or what. Running across a snowfield." Only after I said that could I manage a smile. Thuỷ held up his hands to the front and imitated a dog, making me laugh.

I realized later that the ridiculous things Thuỷ said or did were a trick used by mature, thoughtful kids. Having become adults long before their peers, they performed the part of the most clueless, innocent child. They took it upon themselves to play the carefree fool so that you could lay down your pains through them, forget your burdens for a moment and laugh. Back then, having thought the serious and cynical kids were the mature ones, I had no way of recognizing Thuỷ's thoughtfulness.

"Mom's gonna be here soon. She's taking classes these days, see. She should be done right about now," said Thuỷ. We hadn't talked in so long that he felt a little like a stranger. I didn't go to his house and he didn't come to mine. We kept aloof at school and when we bumped into each other on the way home, we would just exchange nods and walk past coolly. At such moments, Thuỷ was not the boy I knew. He was so much taller now that he didn't even look like a child from a distance. Talking with him just like old times, as if everything was alright, made it seem like a lot of time had passed. We sat side by side on a park bench.

"I didn't mean to put you down that day," said Thuỷ. While I tried to think of what to say, he continued, "I didn't say those things to attack you."

"I'm sorry."

It was only when I blurted out those words that I realized I'd wanted to tell him that for a long time. His large eyes blinked. Every time the wind blew, a ball of snow fell from a branch and crumbled on our heads.

"I'm sorry I didn't know anything," I said slowly. As carefully as if the wind might sweep my words away. I knew those words would change nothing back, but I still wanted to say them. Thuỷ's eyes met mine and he kicked the ground a few times with the tips of his shoes. Then he looked up at me again. He looked embarrassed. His lips slowly parted, from which escaped a white breath that scattered into thin air. He took out a paper bag from his backpack.

"This is for you, Woodstock."

The paper bag contained a comic book. On the cover, Woodstock and Snoopy were sitting on the doghouse roof, grinning at each other. We would never sit together like that anymore, and I would never be called by my silly nickname again.

We sat there talking nonsense until Mrs. Nguyễn came. Why on earth did dog poop keep popping up at this park, no matter how often you cleaned it? How many piles of poop were frozen underneath that white snow? Any mention of poop had once sent us rolling on the floor, but now we couldn't laugh like we used to somehow. Poop jokes weren't funny anymore.

Mrs. Nguyễn saw us sitting together and waved. She sat down beside me.

"When are you leaving?"

"Tomorrow night."

She gazed unresponsively at the trash can. Sheepish, I uncrossed my arms and placed Mom's box on Mrs. Nguyễn's lap.

"Here, my mom wanted me to give you this."

Slowly, she tore off the wrapping paper and opened the box. In it were three sets of scarves, wool hats, and wool mittens that Mom had knitted since the fall. Mom, who is this for? I had asked. Mom's face, when she airily replied that she was just knitting out of boredom, rushed back to me. Mrs. Nguyễn took out the red wool hat and put it on. Other than the fact that it was made of wool, it looked like the narrow-brimmed hat she often wore in the summer. A rose-shaped woolen corsage was knitted onto the hat. She took all the hats, mittens, and scarves from the box and held them up to the sky one by one. As if they were jewels she had to delicately examine in the pale light. She held up a navy blue hat embroidered with a capital *T* in yellow yarn and looked at it for a long time before she pulled it over Thuỷ's head.

"He has a big head so hats don't usually fit him. But . . ." She broke off, shut her mouth tightly, and sniffed. That was the first time I'd seen her swallow back tears. I didn't know how to arrange my face as I sat beside her, having seen her maintain her calm even when she had talked about the war, without the slightest change of expression. Mrs. Nguyễn. I looked at her face.

Large brown eyes and a small nose, the corners of her mouth drooping because she was holding back tears, two vertical wrinkles etched between her brows.

I blew off the ball of snow that had fallen onto her wool hat.

"Xin chào," I said, looking at her small face.

"Xin chào," she echoed.

"Xin chào, Thuỷ," I said a little more loudly. Thuỷ looked at me, nose red and hands in pockets, wearing the navy blue wool hat. I took in that face. "Xin chào," Thuỷ said in a small voice.

Maybe I was hoping for a certain kind of scene. Maybe I wanted to see Mrs. Nguyễn go up to my house and bid my family goodbye, see Mrs. Nguyễn and Thuỷ show my mom how they looked in the hats she knitted for them, see my mom's face looking at them proudly. But there was no such dramatic scene. Not even the most conventional hug, nor any kisses, nor effusive farewell messages. Goodbye, that was all that was said. We got up from the bench and brushed the snow off our coats and walked toward the sidewalk. I crossed the street; Mrs. Nguyễn and Thuỷ did not. They waited until I arrived at my doorstep before they set off. I wouldn't be able to see them once they turned that corner. I stood rooted to my doorstep and watched them stroll away. Once or twice, Thuỷ turned back and looked my way, but he didn't stop walking. They turned the corner, and I could see them no longer. Maybe they'd come back. I crouched down on the doorstep and waited for them. They never came, so I walked to the front of Thuỷ's house. No one was on the street.

Over time, whenever a relationship came to an end, I pondered who had left and who was left behind. Sometimes I was the one who left, sometimes the one left behind, but when a relationship I especially cherished broke down, I wasn't sure who left whom. Both sides left at times, both were left behind at others, the line between leaving and being left often blurred.

Despite going on multiple business trips to Germany, I didn't drop by Plauen. I took pains to avoid the place, even when I happened to be only a two-hour train ride away in Leipzig for ten days. In Plauen, there was a child shivering from the bottom of her soul under parents who despised each other, and there was a cold farewell made without a single hug, and the street on which she cried alone. That's what I thought all this time. That there were people you parted with whom you could see again genially, and relationships you could smile about regardless of how they ended, just from the memory of them. Yet some partings you never wanted to remember, even after a long time, because they lingered as heartbreaks.

I went to Plauen the year after my mom passed away. It was a week after the first anniversary of her death, in early spring when the sun was warm and the breeze chilly. The city was much smaller than I remembered and had fallen into even deeper decline than twenty years earlier, to the point of looking eerily deserted. My old school had turned into a small factory and a few old men were smoking in the backyard, watching me absently. What hadn't changed was the multifamily house I had lived in. The building still stood in the same spot facing the park. I looked up at the third-floor window I had stood glued to as a kid. Remembering how I used to spy on Thuỷ running around the park from behind the window, a smile tugged at the corner of my mouth.

The Snoopy comic that Thuỷ gave me is still on the bookcase in my room. It's a black-and-white comic book, but Woodstock is colored in with bright yellow. Woodstock, the canary that can't fly properly. Whenever I open the book and see the yellow canary, Thuỷ's warm heart, which compelled him to turn over each page and add color to the little bird, feels so close.

Thuỷ's house wasn't hard to find. I sat on the bench across from his house and gazed at the window. Ah, that was the kitchen window. I faintly recalled the view of the park from that window and Mr. Hồ's back as he stood in the kitchen making dinner. The smell of boiling rice and the aroma of coriander that crunched in my mouth as I ate beef stew, the sweetness of Mrs. Nguyễn's rice pudding, the times I spent with Thuỷ leaning against the wall reading Snoopy comics. Those times were still flowing sweetly yet bitterly through the narrow canals of my heart. So were the times my parents and Thuy's—the former struggling not to give up their rocky relationship, the latter struggling not to wound anyone because they themselves were wounded—sang for each other.

When Mom passed, not many people cried for her. "She was always sensitive and gloomy even as a child." "She wasn't particularly brainy." That's how Mom was remembered even by her older and younger sister. I was reminded of how Mrs. Nguyễn had described her as someone with a big heart. Mrs. Nguyễn was the only person to understand what everyone judged to be Mom's sensitive and gloomy temperament as perceptiveness, as a special gift for empathy. Through her affectionate gaze, Mom was seen as someone who deserved to be loved.

Did Mrs. Nguyễn only see the beautiful sides to Mom, and not her weaknesses? She recognized all of her human shortcomings and still let her into her life just the way she was. How preciously Mom must have looked after the piece of heart Mrs. Nguyễn had given her. And when it shattered through no fault of her own, how deep must have been her despair. As far as I know, Mom had trouble making intimate friends after Mrs. Nguyễn. She probably missed her. Mom said she didn't remember those days very well, but for a long time she must have missed Mrs. Nguyễn, who had loved her as her.

At the very least, I should've been a friend that lent her an ear from time to time. I should've let her into my life at least a little. Not because she was my mother, but because she had been a lonely person for so long. I know now that determination or effort is not necessarily repaid in happiness. The fact that Mom couldn't be happy with us didn't imply a lack of responsibility for her life or negligence over herself.

When I got in touch with Mrs. Nguyễn, she kept saying she couldn't believe it was me. "My husband and I still live here. Thuỷ's working in Hamburg." In the face of her elation, I couldn't tell Mrs. Nguyễn all that had happened, but I did have to answer truthfully to her question, "How is your mother?"

A small woman wearing a red wool hat came out the front door and stood across the street from me. I got up from the bench and walked toward the sidewalk. We gazed at each other for a time with a narrow street between us. The traffic light turned green and I crossed the street. I saw in her eyes an unconcealable shock. The thirty-three-year-old me was the spitting image of my mother when she knew her, as if we were the same person. In Mrs. Nguyễn's eyes, I see my mother standing here with me. Mrs. Nguyễn, she calls gladly, and crosses the street. Xin chào, xin chào. We say the words over and over again. As if we have forgotten every other word.

Sister, My Little Soonae

Auntie came to my mom's hospital ward near daybreak. It was still dark, but Mom could instantly make out Auntie's face even in the darkness. She looked exactly as she had at sixteen. Long hair tied back in a ponytail, black horn-rimmed glasses, the polka-dot summer dress she had made herself. Her face serene, Auntie placed a hand on Mom's right knee where she had received an artificial joint implant. When Mom looked at her, Auntie smiled and spoke.

"I see your knee's causing trouble for you, too, Hae Oak. Can you believe it? You're getting old, too, hun."

"How did you find me here, Sister?"

"I missed you, so I flew."

"How can you fly when you don't have wings?"

"Sure I do. Look."

Auntie spread white wings shaped like semicircular fans from her back and flapped around and around the ceiling of the eight-bed ward. Mom watched in awe at first, but the sight struck her as rather funny and she giggled like a child. Satisfied, Auntie folded her wings and descended to the floor.

"It's good to see you, Hae Oak."

"It really is."

"Would it have been better if we'd kept in touch?" Auntie leaned against the hospital bed and quietly gazed down at Mom. "I still feel like we're little kids. But we're grannies on the outside now."

Mom nodded as she stroked the smooth back of Auntie's hand.

Auntie Soonae was the daughter of my grandmother's older cousin. Grandma was looking for a young girl to help out at the alteration shop and summoned Auntie Soonae, who was searching for a job in Seoul. Mom hid behind Grandma and stole glimpses of the girl standing by the water pump.

"Now you have a big sister, too."

Mom liked Auntie Soonae from the moment she saw her standing quietly in the yard. She liked the ring to the word "sister," the affectionate pang it evoked. Why did girls only a few years her senior seem so much older to her as a kid? Mom couldn't even strike up a conversation with Auntie because her heart was beating so fast. Auntie didn't talk much and blushed easily. She was sixteen but was smaller than Mom, who was eleven, so she had to get all her clothes altered down a couple sizes or make her own. If you were looking for the shortest, skinniest sixteen-year-old girl in the neighborhood, it would've been Auntie.

When anything interesting happened at school, Mom's first thought was to tell Auntie about it. She rushed to the alteration shop as soon as school let out, threw down her bag, and poured out stories to Auntie, who listened to Mom's stories while she marked fabrics with chalk, threaded needles, and pedaled the sewing machine.

The alteration shop was a five-minute walk from home, but Mom and Auntie often took the long way on purpose. Auntie would sometimes stand gazing at the high school girls walking home, or pause in front of the stationery store, or pet a dog tied to a telephone pole for a long time. And Mom would watch the sunlight shimmering on Auntie's head. In such moments, time rolled gently on and the strange optimism that everything was going to be okay filled her heart.

Mom had heard from Grandma that Auntie was separated from her parents during the war, and her grandmother, whom she'd lived with ever since, had passed away. Auntie never spoke of those losses, but on days when the work got tough or her mind was troubled, she would talk about the pet dog she'd had back home. Named Bear, the dog had started to live with her after the war. Mom listened closely to the story, since she could count on the fingers of one hand the times Auntie talked about herself.

"Bear was so sick in his last days that he could hardly eat. Still, when I called out, 'Hey, Bear,' he would force his head up and wag his tail. When I said, 'Here, Bear, eat up,' he poked his nose into his food and pretended to eat as if he wasn't sick. I cried in front of Bear then. I sensed that he wasn't just sick, he was dying. I went to the doghouse the next morning to find Bear gone. I cried at school every day for a month after he disappeared. Cried and cried. I thought Bear left the house because I'd stupidly burst into tears in front of him. I blamed myself, thinking he'd gone out to die because I was hurting over his hurting. I shouldn't have let on no matter how sad I was, I shouldn't have cried."

Listening to the story of Bear, Mom imagined herself as Bear and watched Auntie talk to Bear. Here, Bear, eat up. She watched Auntie say that and sob. When she saw Auntie through Bear's heart, Auntie was the most precious person in the world. Long after hearing the story, Mom would still see Auntie through the dead dog's heart sometimes. See how Auntie had lost everyone against her will and still had more to lose.

Mom loved Auntie.

Auntie's husband was Mom's friend Nan's older brother. He fell for Auntie when he saw her in passing and wrote letters to her that were hand-delivered by his sister Nan. Auntie kept his letters in her pocket and read them whenever she visited the toilet or walked home with Mom.

Auntie in those moments was not the girl who worked the sewing machine and dealt with the neighborhood ladies, nor the girl who stooped beside the water pump and beat laundry with a washing paddle. While she read his letters, her face transformed into that of a twenty-two-year-old girl who pined for ordinary love.

Despite Auntie's efforts to keep at bay the emotions rippling inside her and put on a calm front, Mom saw in her face a strange loneliness. A bewildered and scared yet happy face, desperately yearning for something, yet hesitant.

The two of them dated for two seasons and got married.

Auntie and Mom often met at the kalguksu noodle soup joint in front of Mom's workplace. Auntie didn't mumble like she used to and ordered her food in a loud voice. Her eyes shone when she talked. She was dressed in what was surely a brand-new blouse and a skirt that ended above the knee, and wore a deep pink lipstick that brightened up her face.

Auntie plucked out the clam meat from each and every shell in her bowl of noodle soup and doled it into Mom's bowl, while she herself just ate the noodles.

"You shouldn't give away what's yours all the time. Or else you'll make a habit of giving and giving."

Mom scooped up the clam meat Auntie had given her and transferred it back to Auntie's bowl.

"Hae Oak."

"Hmm?"

"I really want to live well. I want my life to go on like this, just the way it is now. Maybe I'm expecting too much, but I really want to try and live a good life."

Auntie said she was taking the high school equivalency exam soon. She was also preparing for pregnancy, and when the baby came, she would give them all the love and opportunity she never got from her parents. Mom felt jealous of a child who wasn't even born yet.

Auntie hesitated for a moment and said, "No one's ever loved me like you have, Hae Oak. You were on my side no matter what, accepted me unconditionally; you understood me. This may sound strange, but you were like a mother to me."

Mom's family had always been cold to Auntie, but she never once let her disappointment show. Not for the family, but out of pride. She had acted utterly unfazed regardless of how they treated her.

"Here, Sister."

Mom handed Auntie a cowhide wallet. It was the first item she had ever purchased in a department store.

"Your wedding gift. Sorry it's so late. Besides, I didn't get you anything after I got my first paycheck."

"I have a wallet. Why are you giving me something this valuable?"

Mom recalled Auntie's hole-ridden wallet. The wallet she had stitched up again and again until it was in tatters.

"*You* have to use it. Don't be stupid and give it to Brother-in-law. This is a present for you, Sister."

"Would it be right for me to use something like this?"

"'Course it is. I'll get you a nicer one later when I earn more money."

Auntie held the wallet in cupped hands as if it were a small animal and petted it gently. Mom sometimes stepped into her memories and watched Auntie in that moment. Looking at the young girl who was beside herself over a mere leather wallet, Mom asked her why she was so stunned and happy over something so trivial. You should've gotten better things, you deserved them, Mom told her.

When Mom arrived at Auntie's house, she found her sitting on the stairs leading down to the kitchen. A blue bruise the size of her palm covered each of her shins, blood pooling under the skin where her arms were scraped. The kitchen floor was littered with stem ends of kimchi, mackerel bones, eggshells, cigarette butts, soaked black beans, bean sprout heads, leek roots, and onion skins. The sun sinking in the west filtered through the tiny kitchen window and shone down on the filthy mess all over the floor.

Leaving Auntie in the kitchen, Mom went inside the bedroom. Underwear was strewn across the floor, and blankets and mats ripped open by a sharp object lay gaping. A foundation case had been smashed, coating the entire floor in powder. Footprints of dress shoes were stamped all over the debris.

Mom poured some water into a rice bowl for Auntie to keep her hydrated, picked up a broomstick, and set about cleaning the bedroom first. Once she finished mopping the floor, she brought Auntie back into the room and laid her down on one of the gutted mats. Auntie was shivering. Mom could have said that this was probably nothing serious, that there was nothing to worry about, but she couldn't speak. She went home to hastily pack some clothes and toiletries and unpacked them at Auntie's house. When she offered to stay at least until Auntie's husband came back, Auntie put Mom's belongings back in her knapsack, tossed it out of the house, and locked the front door.

Mom went to see Auntie every day after work. She knocked on the front door and called her name. She pounded on the bedroom window asking to be let in. She wanted to show Auntie, at least in a small way, that she was not alone. Auntie had no close friends apart from her husband, and she had been told by Mom's parents not to consider them family, to leave and never look back. The fact that Auntie didn't have a single soul to depend on stung Mom's heart. She sat in front of the house, she didn't know for how long. Grandma stood still in the yard watching Mom.

"Soonae left today. The landlord gave me the keys. Told me to clean up the place."

Grandma opened the front door. The closet, television, refrigerator, and other large furniture were gone, while cotton blankets and Auntie's clothes were neatly folded. There were no men's clothes; Auntie had somehow managed to take every last one of them. Grandma bundled Auntie's clothes and abandoned sundries in fabric.

"Soonae doesn't exist anymore. She's got nothing to do with us, and we've no business seeing her from now on, you hear?"

The bundle was bound by a knot too tight to untie. Mom struggled awhile to untie it but gave up and sank to the floor, hugging the bundle for a long time as if it were Auntie. It smelled faintly of mothballs.

"We can help Soonae out financially. That's enough. You making a fuss will do a fat lot of good, why can't you see that? You keep your nose out of it. Please, just stay put."

"The trial hasn't even started yet, why are you treating Brother-in-law like a criminal already?"

"We don't need to hold a trial to know how this case will end. There's talk all over town already. That Soonae's man was acting on the North's orders," Grandma said quietly.

"There's no proof."

"It was in the papers, mind you. They said those riffraff read communist books and listened to radio broadcasts from the North."

"How can you of all people say that, Mother?"

"If the government says so then it must be true. Shut your eyes, shut your ears, just trust 'em. And don't go around calling her your sister or him your brother-in-law. She's not your real sister. Third cousins are barely related anyway. Don't you go blabbing anywhere."

Grandma wrested the bundle from Mom's hands and chucked it into a nearby creek.

"You never thought of her as family, did you? Family was just an excuse to use her."

"That's right. I did it to live. I didn't think she was family. And neither should you from now on. That's how you and I will save our necks."

Grandma had always been a stingy, heartless woman, and this attitude had gotten her through her frustrating life. Mom couldn't understand a person like that, and despised such an attitude, but years later she came to understand the heartlessness to some extent. If you couldn't share someone's pain, if you didn't have the guts to survive a difficult stretch with them, it was better to choose heartlessness over half-hearted affection. That was Grandma's way.

Prosecutors sought the death penalty for eight of the defendants, life imprisonment for seven, a twenty-year prison term for four, and a fifteen-year term for another four. The trial took place a week later, in which the judges accepted the sentences recommended by the prosecutors and every single defendant appealed. According to the papers, not only did these people violate the Presidential Emergency Decrees, National Security Act, and Anti-Communist Act, but they also prepared, conspired, and agitated for an insurrection. Brother-in-law escaped the death penalty and life imprisonment. That was the only comforting news.

Mom wrote a letter that began "Dear Honorable Mr. President" and sent it to the Blue House. She thought that if the president heard people out, he would realize his misunderstanding and correct the injustice suffered by the prisoners. That's how ignorant and naïve twenty-year-old Mom was. She was a little girl who couldn't in her wildest dreams imagine that humanity was capable of framing and killing innocent people to seize even the smallest slice of power.

The appeal was held two months later, and none of the sentences from the first trial were reversed. Those sentenced to death or life imprisonment remained at the Seoul Detention Center, and the rest were transferred to Anyang Prison. Mom attended a Thursday Prayer Meeting organized for the defendants. Families of the defendants, Catholic priests, Protestant ministers, and foreigners were gathered at the Korean Christian Building. They prayed for a public trial instead of a secret military tribunal, then they prayed for the defendants in cold prison cells who were denied visits even by their families.

While Mom ate noodle soup with the people there, she overheard nuggets of their stories. The story of neighborhood children who tied a cord around a four-year-old's neck and dragged her around like a dog, calling her the child of a commie and pretending to shoot her dead, while adults huddled around and watched; the story of someone's little girl who went on a picnic and found ants in her lunchbox placed there by her class-mates; the story of a mother walking home from the grocery store when someone hurled a rock at her and cracked her head open. Namsan . . . When that word came up, everyone fell silent as if by unspoken agreement. If only she could, Mom wanted to take back the letter she had sent to the president and tear it to shreds that instant.

Sister, I'm sorry. Mom said this in her head to Auntie, Auntie whose whereabouts she didn't even know.

Mom came out of the Korean Christian Building and walked, not knowing where she was headed. Soon, she reached Dae-hangno. People were gathered at the square in twos and threes, laughing and talking boisterously. The stories of people who were with her only moments ago seemed as far away as dreams. So did Brother-in-law's benignly smiling face as he said, "my sis-in-law Hae Oak," and Sister's glowing face whenever she was with him. Mom bowed her head.

Mom handed out the Catholic Priests' Association for Justice brochures at her office. Every time she did, the mood suddenly became heavy, and she sometimes heard muffled laughter.

"Miss Lee, be a good girl and save your energy for finding a husband. Take it from someone who knows. The world can screw you over even if you keep your head down, Miss Lee," said the department head, who took great pride in having participated in the April 19 Revolution. He added gently, as if to reason with her, "No matter what you do, nothing'll change. Stay out of this. Stop acting like a child."

Every Thursday Mom went to Myeongdong, where she attended prayer meetings for the recovery of democracy and accompanied the defendants' families to hand out brochures demanding a public trial. She went for the sake of Auntie and her brother-in-law at first, but increasingly she was just drawn there. At rallies, she stood at the farthest corner listening to speeches and briskly brought up the rear at marches. She put the rent she owed her parents into activity funds and supported the Thursday meetings with the bus fares she saved by walking most places.

The executions were carried out eighteen hours after the Supreme Court ruling.

Unaware that the executions had already taken place, the families were on their way to discuss countermeasures to the death sentences when they received the news, and slumped to the ground. Without once being allowed to touch their husbands' and fathers' and sons' faces, without getting to say a simple goodbye or take care, not even a don't worry or don't be scared, without once getting to look into each other's eyes to their heart's content if nothing else, they lost their loved ones, just like that. The state burned the bodies of the executed prisoners without asking permission from the families and sent them the ashes. *I wanted to at least touch his dead body.* Completely spent, one of the wives of the executed men managed to string those few words together. Mom couldn't stay in the room much longer and went outside.

The world sneered at anyone's love for another person, the desperate wish to give one's own life over and over again if it meant saving the life of another. The world said: loving others isn't worth a penny, you weaklings better watch out; what does it matter if those eight nobodies are dead, the law is what we say it is and the commies are who we say they are; when we tell you to kneel you kneel, we can easily kill you by slapping a charge on you, so shut your mouth and do what we say.

They were murdered by the state.

Only when the executions took place did Mom realize that she knew nothing about the world and would never know any better. She cried silently on the bus to work and kept her mouth shut about the matter forever after. People told her she'd finally come to her senses and said, That's how you become an adult. No one thought to examine the bruises inside her. The incident had nothing to do with her, in other people's eyes, and not one of them suspected it had damaged her.

Mom confessed that she became a reticent person from that day on. She said she was ashamed of all the naïve comments she had blurted out about the incident and of her idealistic misconception of the world, that the world's solidity—the impenetrable wall common sense had no hope of piercing—had silenced her. That silence was broken by an unexpected person.

"Hae Oak, are you okay?"

Coffee mug in hand, Mom stood rooted to the spot and stared at him. "What do you mean?" she asked, and left. But the words that had emerged from his cold face stayed with her for a long time. That was the first personal conversation Mom had with Dad, a year after she joined the company.

Dad had lost his first wife the year he turned twenty-five and hadn't dated for five years since. He always had a cold expression on his face, from which Mom could read neither emotion nor thought. Even back when she was busily handing out brochures to her coworkers and explaining the incident, he looked icily at her as usual. That such a man would ask about her well-being made her indignant, but also curious about what he was really thinking.

"She was the kind of person who would grin and bear too much," said Dad.

While her flu was developing into acute pneumonia, Dad's first wife made enough kimchi to last throughout the winter. She went to the hospital only after burying all the pots of kimchi in the yard, but by then it was too late.

"We got married the week after our first date set up by a matchmaker. Since two strangers had suddenly become family, it took us some time to get used to each other. We'd never even walked side by side before. She said she was taught that walking with a man was scandalous. She was a bit of a chump. I liked that. Her gullible side. Otherwise she wouldn't have lived with me. And my goodness, she made so much kimchi, I ate only kimchi for every meal but there was still plenty left. It was really tasty, though. I thought she must feel cheated. Not even getting to taste the kimchi she'd worked so hard to make, the chump."

Dad related such details with the impassive face of someone discussing a meeting agenda. Listening to him speak without pretense or exaggeration, Mom was reminded of Auntie Soonae. Mom and Dad ate dinner together after work and headed to the middle school field behind the office. They sat on the bleachers and talked, almost in whispers. For the first time, Mom broached a subject she had avoided since the executions.

"This country killed people who were innocent."

"I know. It was judicial murder."

"Then why was your face like that before?"

"Hae Oak, in my hometown . . . soldiers rounded up our women and children toward the end of the war and shot them all dead, for 'fraternizing' with the North. After gathering everyone at the school field, the soldiers lined them up and slaughtered them. My mother survived because she hid in the shed hugging me, but she carried a sense of guilt with her for the rest of her life. She told me we survived by luck. From when I was a kid, I kept thinking about why those people died and I lived.

How people could kill other people so easily. How they could kill a newborn infant while the mother watched. How people could sweep these things under the rug so easily like they never happened and keep pressing forward. To find what ahead? What exactly lay ahead to make us forget what people did to people and go about life as usual? All I did was think. Since I did absolutely nothing, even if someone accused me of fraternizing with the world, I would not deny it. I don't have the courage you have, Hae Oak."

Mom and Dad didn't have a ceremony but registered their marriage and moved in together. Mom's family opposed her marriage to a man who was much older and whose fortune and résumé were nothing to boast about. And she was to be his second wife, no less. Mom became an object of disgrace to her family, who severed ties with her. It was around then that Auntie Soonae got back in touch with Mom.

"I hope I didn't startle you, phoning out of the blue? I called your office and they told me your home phone number. Congratulations. On getting married."

There was a click as the payphone swallowed a coin.

"Hey, I had a baby in January."

"You did?"

"Come see us in Anyang sometime."

Despite hearing that Auntie had a baby, Mom couldn't bring

herself to congratulate her. The fact that Auntie gave birth on her own had stunned Mom into silence. It was only after she hung up that she realized Auntie must have wanted to be congratulated by her. That must be the only reason, if any, for Auntie to call her up again.

Mom met Auntie a few times in front of the Anyang intercity bus terminal. Every time they met, Auntie couldn't look up at Mom's face properly. She stole sidelong glances at her and quickly looked away if their eyes met. When she talked, her eyes were fixed on the tips of her fingernails, her toes poking out of her slippers, a cigarette butt on the street, the gauze towel for the baby. Her voice had become smaller than before, so Mom had to ask the same questions multiple times. Her heels were covered in white cracks and blood blisters.

Auntie was proud of her daughter. The baby was sweet tempered and slept soundly at night; she could stand, if only briefly; she didn't cry very much; and she knew how to wait while her mother worked. While Auntie talked about such things, her voice grew confident and her hunched shoulders straightened. She was putting all her hopes in the child. She wasn't wishing for the child to grow up a certain way or to become anything in particular; the mere fact of the child staying alive by her side seemed to give Auntie the energy to live. Mom thought that this child, stuck to Auntie's back taking tiny breaths, was Auntie's heart beating outside her body.

Auntie didn't mention what had happened in the past year and

Mom didn't ask, either. Auntie did request, however, that Mom not visit her brother-in-law in prison. Auntie explained that mailing him books to read was enough and that it was hard for him to see old faces. *He got a little injured in there.* That was all Auntie would say.

Mom had heard at Thursday Prayer Meetings about how the people dragged to Namsan were tortured. She had heard about people whose eardrums were blown out and ribs were crushed and shinbones snapped. Not because they were hit by a car or fell off a cliff, but because another person did that to them. Mom couldn't look Auntie in the face when she calmly said that her husband now had a limp.

Auntie and Mom didn't talk about the people who were murdered. Auntie said she had attended the final trial but could say no more. She needed to talk about something else, change the subject, but the thought seemed to have knocked all else out of her mind. Mom talked about herself in such moments, albeit awkwardly. She listed every lousy part of her marriage and mentioned being estranged from her parents' side of the family to suggest that she was having a tough time, too. She said these things when she was in fact pretty happy, thinking that letting even a little of that happiness show would make Auntie feel deprived in comparison. She realized only much later that her behavior was an insult to someone experiencing pain.

Mom went to see Auntie twice a month at first, but her visits to Anyang turned into once a month, once every two months, then once every season. In the occasional phone call, they made superficial conversation because they had nothing else to talk about. Auntie was no longer honest with Mom nor Mom with Auntie. Mom tried to tread carefully on only the parts of Auntie's heart untouched by scars, as if on thin ice, and Auntie made an effort not to bring up painful subjects lest Mom pity her in the slightest. Mom didn't even know what exactly Auntie did for a living in Anyang. The attitudes they adopted out of consideration for each other slowly drove them apart, and the bond they had forged during the time they lived together could no longer sustain their relationship. They grew even more distant when Mom was pregnant and had a baby. She hesitated to share the details of how her body was changing or how she was preparing to give birth, afraid that discussing her pregnancy would remind Auntie of her darkest days. She would think about calling Auntie, but the longer she put it off, the harder it became to call. "Dear Sister . . ." she would start her letter, but run out of things to say and give up.

As Mom's life settled down, Auntie became burdensome to her. Auntie made her feel uncomfortable. The wan face with no makeup, the pinky toes poking out of her cheap sandals, the unconfident look and voice, the single-minded devotion to her child, the dried tear stains on the lenses of her glasses, her constant attempts to pick up the bill despite being strapped for cash, the nonchalance with which she pretended she didn't need help, her inability to speak up about the injustice her husband suffered.

There was Mom, who thought, Sister, your attitude only vindicates the people who say Brother-in-law is guilty. Then there was Auntie, who tried her utmost to react warmly to Mom's cold face and tell Mom in a roundabout way, I desperately need you. Auntie's sweaty face on her rare visits to Seoul, as she cradled Mom's son and looked sadly at him. Those eyes. Her stupid repertoire about the dead dog.

"Hae Oak, remember my old dog Bear? I still think about him, you know."

Mom did not want to hear any more of Auntie's stories.

She did not initiate contact with Auntie, and answered coldly when Auntie called. Auntie stopped calling Mom before long. The fact that Mom found her burdensome distressed her, but it distressed Mom just as much for a long time. Even now, Mom wonders how she could have ever forsaken Auntie Soonae. She thinks about why it was so hard for her to look squarely at someone who had suffered pain beyond her imagination. Some people break up after a big fight, but there are also people who drift incrementally apart until they can't face each other anymore. The latter stay longer in your memory.

In her early twenties, Mom figured she would be able to make special friends at any point in her life. She vaguely expected to go on having lots of people whom she could treat honestly and openly, like the relationships she had struck up in her youth. But no new relationship could replace those she'd lost. The most important people turned up surprisingly early in life. After a certain point, she found it difficult to turn even the first page of relationships that her younger self would've entered with relative ease. People locked their hearts at some point in their lives, as if everyone had agreed to do so. Then they made acquaintances outside those locks, with people who would never hurt them or be hurt by them, formed savings groups among themselves, vacationed with other married couples, or went hiking together. Telling each other that they never wanted to go back to being twenty. Saying they were pretty clueless back then, weren't they?

Mom saw Auntie one more time. It was the winter her brother-in-law was released from jail.

Auntie's house was on the second floor of a small building behind a shoe factory. Mom climbed the iron staircase and came upon a closed roller shutter. Standing before it, she called Auntie. Footsteps sounded and the shutter moved up. Auntie gave Mom a strained smile and invited her in, asking whether the place wasn't too hard to find. The room smelled moldy and Auntie opened the window as soon as Mom stepped in. A cold draft rushed into the room, but Mom didn't ask for the windows to be closed, because she felt that Auntie was trying as she might to get rid of the smell. The floor shook every time a car rolled by outside.

Auntie's daughter sat behind a small foldable table doing homework for the holidays. The soles of the child's socks were caked in glossy black grime. The child said hello to Mom, avoiding her face. Brother-in-law sat across from the child. He was sitting like a still life object, legs outstretched and eyes staring at a corner of the room. He was so emaciated that his skin barely covered his bones. He hadn't simply lost weight; his entire frame seemed to have shrunk. His eyes looked unnatural, as if he were keeping them wide-open on purpose, and an odd smile played across his face.

"Hae Oak is here, honey. My little sister Hae Oak. You remember, right?" Auntie said to him warmly, though in a tone that she might use on a very young child, and he crinkled his face in a smile at Mom.

"Put this on at least, sweetie."

Auntie handed a blue jacket to her husband, who was in long johns. Bit by bit he tried to put on the jacket but to no avail. Fitting his hand into a sleeve seemed too strenuous for him, and his fingertips were trembling. Mom glanced at Auntie, who averted her gaze.

Auntie's daughter took his hand and pulled it through a sleeve for him. She pushed up his glasses, which had slipped down the bridge of his nose, and tucked in his other arm. Once both arms were in, she skillfully buttoned up the jacket. The child grabbed the black sweatpants that lay crumpled in a corner of the room and helped him into them. He was passively receiving his daughter's assistance like an infant, yet he glared at the door as if he were refusing to meet her eyes.

"I got fried chicken. You used to love this stuff, Sister."

Mom took out the paper-bagged chicken from a plastic bag. The savory aroma of fried chicken, mixed with the moldy odor of the house, turned into the rank smell of stale pork. Auntie spread newspaper on the floor, while Mom ripped open the paper bag and laid out the chicken on top.

"It's still hot," Auntie said as she brought to her mouth a chunk of meat she'd torn off the moment she laid eyes on the chicken. This was a strange sight to Mom, having been used to an Auntie who, when eating together, always invited others to eat first before she started eating. Auntie chewed on the meat as though she'd been famished for days, wheezing and gasping for breath. She devoured the meat like no one else was in the room, like someone who knew no shame, dribbling saliva.

Mom gestured to Auntie's daughter to come and eat. When she held out the last remaining drumstick, the child snatched it from her hand and blew on it a few times before she brought it to her father's mouth. He turned his head away, but she held the drumstick to his lips again without a word. He flailed his arms and scowled. Auntie, meanwhile, was gnawing the cartilage off a chicken bone as if she couldn't see anything. Chicken fat mingled with saliva glistened at the corners of her mouth. The child persistently tried to push the chicken into his mouth. The instant she plucked a chunk of meat with her hand and forced it into his mouth, his floundering body went still.

His urine oozed out onto the floor. Hot urine trickled past

Mom's fingers and stockings, past the hem of her dress, soaking the newspaper spread out on the floor and soiling the chicken. How could so much water leak out of a person's body? He sat motionless, growing steadily wetter. Because the floor sloped to Mom's side, the urine reached the wall opposite him. The child fetched a yellowed rag and began mopping up the floor. Auntie hastily transferred the few pieces of chicken untouched by urine onto the small table and looked at Mom. She seemed to have finally come to her senses, and her ears growing crimson.

"Oh dear, your nice clothes are ruined. Go on and wash up at the water pump first. I'll get him washed and changed in the meantime."

Mom went to the water pump and rinsed his urine off her hands, then rubbed her stockings and the hem of her dress clean. She shivered as she pulled back on the stockings she had washed in cold water. The smell of soybean soup boiling in a neighbor's kitchen wafted over. Mom wasn't sad. Nor was she enraged at the people who'd broken the man. Quite simply, she did not like this house. She did not want to see Auntie's child even, that little child. All she wanted was to get out of this place and crawl into her clean and comfortable home, into the safety of her blankets. She wanted to see her child, who had on clean socks. When she returned to the room, she and Auntie had trouble carrying on a conversation. Auntie apologized over and over again for not having a new pair of stockings that Mom could change into.

"You should get going," Auntie said, her face tightening.

"But I only just got here . . . ," Mom said insincerely.

"This is why I told you not to come. Please, go," Auntie said with her eyes on her husband. Mom clutched her handbag and got up awkwardly. Perhaps a large truck was passing by because the floor shook violently as if it might collapse. He saw Mom saying goodbye and mechanically returned the gesture, the corners of his grinning lips convulsing.

"I can't walk you out too far," Auntie said as she came out of the room. Not knowing what to say, Mom kept her mouth closed and looked at Auntie for a moment, waved, turned around, and walked off.

"Hae Oak," Auntie called after her. Auntie was standing with her shoulders huddled and her hands in her pants pockets. The carelessly chopped bob, the bloated figure almost completely concealing her neck, the gruffer voice. Sister, I hate you, I hate your house, I hate everything about you.

Auntie stood just like that and gazed quietly at Mom before she spoke. Her voice was too small for Mom to hear. Mom shouted back that she couldn't hear her very well, could she repeat what she said?

"I said I'm not always like this. Really, I don't always live like this."

Mom nodded, then turned on her heels and once more walked away.

Hae Oak, take care.

Mom pretended not to hear her and strode forward with her arms crossed. Not once did she look back, but she knew Auntie would stand there until she was out of sight. *Hae Oak, take care.* Auntie said those words as if pushing a beached boat out onto a lake.

As Grandma had wished, Mom had nothing to do with Auntie for the rest of her life. But she still thought of her sometimes. She thought of her when she saw the setting sun through the kitchen window while she cooked dinner, or when she saw mothers carrying on their backs a baby that looked no more than a year old. She sped up when she happened to pass the Korean Christian Building or Myeongdong Cathedral, and while she did consider contacting Auntie again a few times in her life, she never acted on it. Time recorded Auntie as someone who had once come and gone in her life, a fact she chose to accept.

Mom had heard the story that immediately after death, a person's soul went to see someone very important to them who was far away. When Auntie came to Mom's hospital ward as her sixteen-year-old self, Mom knew that she had already been forgiven by Auntie long ago. Auntie's face, as she looked at Mom, had the same lonely, translucent glow it had had when she read her husband's love letters once upon a time. Every time Mom's gaze touched Auntie, she became smaller and smaller, like soap dissolving in water.

"You're growing lighter, Sister," Mom said to Auntie, who had shrunk to the size of a palm.

"Hae Oak, remember."

The smaller Auntie's body grew, the deeper her voice rang.

"No one can kill us."

Mom imitated the shape of Auntie's moving lips, watching Auntie talk perched on one of the partitions in the ward. No one can kill us. Auntie nodded with her slender neck and little head.

"Don't forget that, Hae Oak."

Sunlight streamed down from the window and Auntie, now the size of a thumb, let the light carry her away. For a long while, Mom's gaze lingered on the stream of sunlight from the window. Then she felt her right knee, on which Auntie had placed her hand. It really wasn't a dream. I was asleep on the trundle bed, but Mom shook me awake and said that a sister from her childhood had just come by the room to see her. I was as astonished by her reaction as I was scared and didn't want to hear any more of the matter, but there was no stopping Mom once the words started pouring out of her.

Although Mom was absolutely convinced that everything she experienced the day Auntie came to see her was real, she couldn't be sure about that momentary feeling she'd had of being forgiven by Auntie. That is, until she saw a photograph of two girls in an old leather wallet Auntie had left her.

The small, scrawny girl who looks the younger of the two is hugged from behind by the tall girl. The small girl is wearing a polka-dot dress she made; the tall girl is wearing shorts and a T-shirt with a stretched neckline. They are standing in front of a stone wall, beaming without a trace of shadow. This was the day they went to explore the now-gone Seoul National Museum. The laminated photograph was found in an inside pocket of the wallet, which was tattered and glossy at the corners. Mom couldn't say much to Auntie's daughter, who had come to deliver the wallet. She could only gaze at the photograph and quietly whisper, *Sister, my little Soonae.*

Hanji and Youngju

I *think of you as I watch the light reflecting off a glacier.*

A hundred white nights.

Light intoxicates people but also keeps them awake. Here, my eyes are open yet I am dreaming. It is as if you are standing in front of that glacier, your body under the sun giving off a bluish hue.

In this isolation with nothing but light, I intend to drill into the heart of Antarctica and discover the six hundred and fifty thousand years of memories etched into the ice. I know I don't have the courage or the strength to do it.

I've come here nonetheless.

Listening to stories of Antarctica and glaciers, white nights and black days, I thought maybe you weren't in Nairobi but here, in this

land of ice. You, standing still in front of a brilliant glacier—that
vision I had of you has led me to this icy continent.

I want to give this notebook to you.

Europe was in the middle of World War II when a young,
twenty-five-year-old man founded this monastery. He had traveled the remote villages of France in search of a site for the monastery before coming across a small, run-down village near Lyon.
The young had left, and the only ones left behind were the old,
who were enduring the loneliness of war. When he stopped by
the village, an old woman invited him over and said, "Thank you
for coming to this desolate place."

Unable to forget her words, he later returned to the village,
bought an abandoned house, and opened a monastery. It was
called a monastery, but he was the only monk there and scraped
by raising two goats.

He was a gentle, shy man who pursued a simple life consisting
of prayer, labor, and rest. He didn't think a vengeful, jealous, and
angry God existed, believing the only thing God could give people was love. He had faith in God's love despite knowing what
people did to other people during war. In his monastery, he hid
Jews fleeing the Nazis during World War II, and afterward con-
cealed escaping German POWs.

Those who wanted to live with him came to his shabby home

and took their monastic vows. He had a Protestant background, but among those who sought to join his order were Catholics including priests, Russian Orthodox Christians, Greek Orthodox Christians, and Anglicans. The brothers of various denominations prayed three times a day with short, repetitive songs sung in the Russian Orthodox Church, while a brother who had studied music composed new songs of a similar form each year. Some of the songs were written in Latin, some in German, French, Russian, or Polish. These songs along with ten minutes of silence made up their thrice-a-day communal prayer routine. In the morning, the brothers read a passage of Scripture, meditated in silence, and received the Eucharist. They took no donations or gifts of any kind, and instead raised funds the monastery needed by making pottery and writing books.

As a rule, they did not turn away visitors; anyone who wished to pray and labor was welcome to stay. People from all over Europe flocked to the monastery in the summer, over four thousand in some weeks. It was difficult for the hundred-odd brothers to receive all of them, and as visitors increased, long-term guests helped the brothers host new ones. What had started out as an abandoned house in a dreary village became a monastery attracting more than a hundred thousand visitors each year.

Most of the volunteers in the beginning were European and stayed at the monastery anywhere from a month to two years. Eventually, the monastery began inviting volunteers, sponsoring flights for twenty-somethings from developing nations who, for distance or cost reasons, hadn't been able to make the trip to France. A pair of volunteers each from countries across Africa, Asia, Latin America, and more were invited to live, work, and pray at the monastery for the three months of summer when it was busiest.

I still don't know why I stayed there for so long.

Seven months, to be exact, when I had planned to spend only a week. It was during my first communal prayer that I realized I couldn't leave the place in just a week. I had been in the middle of a two-week trip in France. The monastery helped me get a visa and I arranged to take time off from graduate school.

I was twenty-seven at the time.

This made me the oldest of the girls in the monastery, which only chose long-term volunteers aged from nineteen to under thirty. The majority of them were twenty-three- or twenty-four-year-olds fresh out of college, trying to find their way. I'm twenty-seven, I would say, and be met by a short silence. My parents, my sister who'd had a baby right before I left, my thesis adviser, and my labmates all reacted the same way. You had to be a go-getter in your twenties more than any other time, where being a go-getter meant building a safe career as quickly as possible or die trying.

"Do you have any idea what you're doing?" my big sister had said. "You're letting your life go to waste. The stupidest kind of waste. If you do whatever you want in your twenties, you'll end up like Mom and Dad, never owning their own home. Even if you work under someone else your whole life and take orders till your hands look like feet, you still won't have a coin to spare for your child's wedding. I thought at least you had a goal when you told me you were going to grad school, that you wanted to become a professor. Why else did you invest your time and money? What would your professors and classmates think? Seriously, you know nothing about the world. You should at least have a degree if you don't have savings. Keep sitting on your ass like that and you'll see. You'll end up a nobody. You'll have a life where you'll never get to cradle a child that came out of you."

I agreed with my sister. The fear bordering on rage in her voice was my long-time master. That fear had driven me since childhood and raised me into an adult who didn't look so precarious on the outside. It had urged me not to be me, to never stop evolving into a better person. If I didn't change, if I didn't improve, I would be erased from this world.

Yet I chose to stay there.

My boyfriend was silent.

In our final call, when I told him I would remain at the monastery and I wasn't sure for how long, he had let out a short sigh and said, "Fine." That was it. He hung up before I could say sorry.

We had resorted to every means, except fighting, to tolerate each other. We didn't even have the desire to vent our emotions or bad-mouth each other to see how the other would react. You would need at least a shred of affection for fights to happen. I did not hate him, nor he me. His words and actions didn't hurt me. Mine didn't hurt him, either, I think. We didn't know how to be horrible to each other. But looking back, not even knowing how to be horrible to each other—that unawareness—was the most horrible part.

We had been politely covering each other's eyes. In the end, I took my hand off his eyes first, and we split up cleanly. That farewell proved there was no love left between us because the last moment of lovers was never supposed to be so clean. We had simply moved from one dot to another.

I received a text from him four weeks after our final call.

Thank you for letting me date you these past three years. I'm sorry, but let's stop seeing each other now.

He always said I was "letting" him date me. The word flustered me, made me despise him a little, and above all made me take him for granted. He would've used that turn of phrase with not just me but anyone he dated. Always underestimating himself, he was stingy with self-approval to the point of being cruel rather than humble.

I had become his first ever girlfriend when he was twenty-seven.

"No girl's shown interest in me before. Dating was only possible in my dreams."

He wasn't exceptionally handsome, but he was likable enough

at first glance, very knowledgeable, played the piano well, and was even a good kisser. Still he believed, deep down, that he could never be loved. He never expressed that thought out loud, but he planted similar messages in his language and behavior over the three years I dated him, so that I wound up getting brainwashed by his belief. How had that been possible?

There was a time when I had felt much more affectionate toward him than I would, later, toward Hanji. But my affections vanished at one point and the man who stood before me seemed like a large paper doll. A different kind of sadness than when love is broken.

How could that have happened?

There was a lot I wanted to say to him, but I held back. Simply, I texted him saying I was sorry for leaving Korea without consulting him and thanked him, too, for our time together. It was an indifferent breakup, though I remember crying inexplicably.

I had been at the monastery for four months when I went to pick up Hanji and Caro, who had flown in from Kenya. Since few of the volunteers knew how to drive or were familiar with the area, I was tasked, along with Theo, to fetch the newly invited volunteers. It was June, a busy time when volunteers landed in Lyon in droves. I had picked up volunteers from Mexico, Madagascar, and Vietnam so far. It was a pleasant task. How liberating it felt to drive an old jalopy and soak in the scenery outside.

The moment Hanji appeared at the arrivals gate, my gaze easily gravitated toward him. He was tall; even at a glance I could tell he was at least six foot two. He wore long chinos and leather shoes despite the heat. He beamed as he walked toward me and Theo, like we were old friends he hadn't seen in years. The girl walking next to Hanji introduced herself as Caro. The four of us hugged and started talking. Hanji, Theo, and Caro spoke in rapid French. I took Caro's small backpack and strode ahead.

"You don't speak French?" Caro asked, and I replied in English that I didn't. "Not even listening?" I shook my head. Caro turned back to Hanji and Theo and addressed them in English. "Let's talk in English. Youngju doesn't speak French." Theo said he had used French unconsciously and apologized for not being considerate of me.

The day was clear, the jalopy was creaking along, everyone except me seemed to hit it off from the start and chatted excitedly in French until they, conscious of me, switched to English before eventually reverting to French. Asking them to speak in English seemed petty, so I drove in silence. I felt left out, but, unwilling to admit it, I simply turned on the radio and kept my eyes on the road.

A brother from Kenya was waiting for us at the monastery. Hanji and Caro smiled broadly, as they had when they first saw us, and ran to the brother to give him a hug. The three of them walked over to a table set up for them. I said goodbye and was about to leave when Hanji said, "Youngju, thank you," looking steadily at me.

"See you later," I said, went outside, and was greeted by a shower of rain.

There had been twenty long-term volunteers when I first arrived, but that number swelled to forty by the time Hanji came. Thirty girls, ten guys. The girls shared a two-story building on the monastery grounds. Four slept in each room, and there was a cafeteria and common room on the second floor. The guys were lodged in an old house outside the monastery's front gates. In front of the house was an enormous lime tree whose flowers gave off a heady scent that filled the evening air. We called the guys the "Tilleul Boys" since they lived next to a lime tree. The Tilleul Boys would loudly greet the occasional passerby from their balcony.

Every Saturday morning, a week's worth of work was assigned to each of us. We had morning, midday, and evening duties amounting to about six hours of labor per day. They were things like cooking in the big kitchen, putting up tents for visitors, cleaning, doing dishes, welcoming visitors, tidying up the church, and for those of us with a driver's license, driving trucks or sedans so old it was a wonder their engines started.

Communal prayers took place three times a day. They began when the brothers sat down at the center of the church building. The church was somewhat basic, like a school auditorium, and had no chairs. Everyone sat on an old carpet covering the floor and prayed. The long-term volunteers sat together in their designated spots behind the brothers. Hanji showed up at the church for the first time on the day he arrived, for evening prayer. He sat at the right end of my row. He looked comfortable in his blue crew-neck T-shirt and shorts. Having just finished doing the dishes, I removed my boots, sat barefoot on the floor, and began to nod off. After all the brothers left, people who wished to sing stayed back and sang together. I was still dozing with my head tilting to one side.

"Youngju."

Hanji, who had sat some distance away, was now right beside me. The volunteers he'd sat with had all left. He was looking at my face as he picked up and dropped my boots repeatedly.

That was when I saw Hanji's face close up for the first time. His skin had a sheen to it without a single wrinkle, and his large eyes were clear, like a child's. He had white teeth and half of a front tooth had chipped off. A long neck extended from the crew-neck shirt. He smelled like summer grass.

"Tired?" asked Hanji.

"Aren't you? You traveled all the way from Africa."

"Not at all. Hey, can you show me where the store is? I didn't bring a toothbrush."

I slipped my feet into the boots and headed out of the church. A group of long-term volunteers from Latin America was chatting animatedly by the wall opposite the church. Hanji spoke to them in Spanish with a bright smile. As if he had known them all his life.

"Youngju. Were you mad in the car before?"

"No."

"I think you were. Because we were talking only in French."

"That's not true. I was just tired because I have a lot of work these days. See? I can't talk well in English, either."

Hanji shook his head and said, "No, I completely understand you."

Hanji had said "I completely understand you" to mean "I understand everything you're saying."

"Youngju, you know what? This is my first time abroad. And my first time meeting a Korean. You're my first Korean, Youngju."

"You've never seen other Asians?"

"No. I've seen Chinese people walking by in Nairobi, but I never got to talk to them. This is pretty cool and fun, Youngju."

There were a number of high tables in front of the store. People stood around them munching chips or drinking Coke. Under the lamplight of the vacant lot adjoining the store, Hanji's face looked even more foreign to me. I had never met anyone who looked like him. My face probably looked just as foreign to him.

"What do you do?" he asked.

"I'm learning geology at grad school."

"Geology?"

"Studying the Earth's body. Geologists measure the Earth's age, find out what organisms used to live on it, predict volcanic eruptions and earthquakes. They study rocks and glaciers, too."

"Which one of those do you study?"

"I study climates of the past. I recently did research on East Asian climates in the past two thousand years."

"How?"

"By analyzing stalagmites in caves."

"What are stalagmites?"

"The slimy horns growing in caves," I said, pointing at my ice cream cone.

"Ah, I know what those are." Hanji laughed. "By the way, were you also invited here?"

"No. I was going to stay here for just a week. A week turned into two, which turned into three. I don't know how long I'll be here. I took time off from school, I have no plan. I'm twenty-seven. I know I shouldn't be here."

"Why not?" Hanji asked.

"Because running away isn't right. Because I need to take charge of my own life."

"It's okay, Youngju," said Hanji.

That I decided to stay here on impulse, abandoned my responsibilities, was living in a monastery, everything—it was okay.

Hanji's face shone as he said those words. I had never seen such an expression before. It wasn't the face of someone trying to comfort me, nor that of someone offering empty clichés. Neither was it the face of an adult who couldn't even smile without feeling self-conscious. Hanji's face was simply, naturally, relaxed.

When I entered the insular society of grad school, I was

frequently advised to be wary of others. My lack of caution in dealing with people at school was, apparently, very childish. I was given constant warnings that women in particular needed to be careful about how they were perceived, that their future as a researcher was doomed once people started disparaging them behind their back.

And I played by those rules pretty well. I took an active part in both class and fieldwork; I attended socials, where I laughed and talked till late. And yet, on my way home, I would find myself crying for no reason.

My face, with the wrinkle on my brow. In photographs of me smiling, one corner of my mouth is always higher than the other, making my face look lopsided. My smile looks far from natural, closer to a frown, in fact. Ever since I became aware of it, I couldn't look people in the eye when I talked to them.

But that day, I talked to Hanji without avoiding his gaze. And I didn't even realize I wasn't averting my eyes.

Hanji said he was a vet in Nairobi. He usually treated cows and goats on farms. When he was studying veterinary medicine, he had participated in a project that cared for two orphaned rhinos for nine months before sending them back into the wild.

"Their names were Howie and Gloria. We fed them two liters of powdered milk dissolved in water for every meal. We dug a pit in the earth and filled it with water to make them a mud pool. They knew how to bathe in it even though we never taught them. They grew attached to me. They would follow me around everywhere like shadows, look sweetly at me, signal to me that they trusted me entirely. The day was nearing when we'd release them into the wild after their rehabilitation ended, and I didn't have the heart to look at their faces. I felt like I was betraying them, these babies who believed in me and liked me so much. Wouldn't they feel abandoned and sad? I was also scared they might die. Yes, they were rehabilitated, but they were bound to be behind in things, compared to the ones that grew up in the wild. We held a small party on the last day and gave each other a pat on the back. For raising the babies well. That conversation made me tear up."

Hanji's eyes reddened.

"I couldn't believe I was parting with them, I felt like I was doing something awful. I even said I wasn't sure if we were doing the right thing. Then another volunteer told me, that's just what *we* think, we shouldn't keep them from their happiness by imposing a human point of view on them. That we should distinguish love from attachment, that wanting to keep wild animals by my side wasn't real love. On the day of farewell, we placed them in a cage and drove a little way off to release them. I made to turn back, but they kept looking my way. I told them not to look and to just go forward. But they kept looking back. You know something, though? Even as they were looking back, they went forward. Slowly they walked into the prairie with their backs turned to us."

The store closed up while we talked and only a few people remained in the darkness.

"I still think of Howie and Gloria. I'm a human so I have no way to know how rhinos feel, but I try my best to imagine the prairie they'll experience. I'm sure it'll be a better place than the cramped training grounds."

Hanji also told me about his experience of treating sick animals. Some animals that seemed utterly hopeless ended up surviving, some that he thought were easily treatable worsened without warning and died. Whenever that happened, the thought that he had perhaps killed an animal that would have otherwise lived filled him with guilt; he still felt that way now, but all he could do was try his best, though he was learning that his best might not always guarantee success.

"I like animals, too," I said, "but I'd never dreamed of becoming a vet because I thought watching sick animals might be too painful. I didn't have the heart to watch dying animals."

"I understand," Hanji said.

By then we were the only ones left in that vacant lot next to the store.

I didn't get to talk to Hanji in private for some time after that. I saw him three times a day at the church, but we only exchanged nods since we sat so far apart. Hanji had become close with the male volunteers and always hung out with them. Hi, Hanji. When I greeted him, the people invariably by his side started up a conversation with me.

I moved tents and bedsheets by car or cleaned the guesthouses where the brothers' families were staying, while Hanji usually worked in the big kitchen. He made mashed potatoes, mixed cocoa or black tea powder into a large pot full of water, and carried them to the distribution station. From a distance, I'd watch him deliver the food. I began to take lingering walks near the warehouse once I discovered I could see him there before morning prayers.

He worked hard without ever slacking off. He carried gunnysacks, he sprayed water on the floor and scrubbed it with a brush, and he tidied the distribution station. When he was doing something, he seemed completely engrossed in it. I liked to watch him work, but it occurs to me now as I write this that he probably knew I was hovering around him. I made a roof with my hands to block the sun, squinting to see his face.

We had Bible study twice a week.

It took place in an area usually open only to the brothers, in a small house next to the main church. The front of the house was densely lined with dahlia and lavender flowers.

Bible study consisted of an internal analysis on the Bible text itself and an external one using the historical context in which the text was written. A brother explained how the writing of the Bible was influenced by the beliefs or culture of the authors' times, then the volunteers asked him questions as they read the text critically.

"It is interesting that the Bible gives no detailed account of life after death. But what we know for certain is that the soul does not die, and continues to exist in a different state. After death, the soul is no longer affected by the restriction of the body, so it wouldn't be an overstatement to say that we, who have yet to die, know nothing of life after death," said the brother.

"But doesn't the Bible mention Heaven and Hell?" asked Caro.

"The Bible mentions Heaven but does not describe it in detail. Frankly, it is a place that we, as we are now, cannot perceive or imagine," the brother replied.

"I agree that human perception is limited. But I don't know if we can't imagine it. Is there anything humans can't imagine? Does imagination have a limit?" Caro asked again.

"I cannot say for sure. But whatever we imagine, I believe that Heaven will be beyond that. As neither time nor space would exist there, you could say Heaven is the soul's state of being," said the brother.

The bell rang, signaling the start of evening prayer, so the class wrapped up there. It occurred to me during evening prayer that I had never thought about the afterlife before. I had just been overwhelmed by the idea of eternity. In Hell or in Heaven, the idea of eternity was suffocating.

To have no end.

On our way back to the dormitory after evening prayer, I asked Caro, "What do you think about the conclusion that Heaven is the soul's state of being beyond our imagination?"

Caro was silent for a moment, then she said, "I'm not sure."

"What kind of place do you think Heaven might be?"

"I'm not sure, but I think it'll be a different place from this world. A state of only loving and being loved. You can laugh and say I'm being naïve," said Caro.

"If life after death is eternal, why does *this* life exist when it's just a fleeting moment compared to eternity? Is Heaven supposed to be compensation for a life like this?"

"A life like this?" Caro looked searchingly at me.

I said no more to Caro. I didn't tell her that I had been longing to disappear once I die—no, that I was wishing I hadn't existed in the first place. That that would've been better than enduring all of life and entering Heaven.

"Oh, Youngju." Caro said my name and patted my back.

There were several villages near the monastery, big and small. Some of the visitors went there and drank wine over raucous conversation and laughter, but to the villagers the revelry was unbearable noise pollution. As there was often trouble in the nighttime especially, a few volunteers had to stand at the mouth of the roads leading to villages and stop the visitors attempting to go on their nocturnal escapades. This job was called "night guard" duty.

That was the first time I was assigned the same job as Hanji.

A total of ten night guards patrolled five zones, two in each area, from nine to eleven o'clock. Hanji and I were paired up and for two weeks we were responsible for Zone A, the mouth of the road to the largest village near the monastery. The sun hadn't fully set even at nine o'clock and the sky looked like a lake, a dizzying mix of orange, pink, and inky hues. The scent of lime tree blossoms wafted over in the cool breeze. That evening, Hanji and I sat on a bench watching people return to the family lodgings.

Families were housed in off-site accommodations from which they cycled back and forth to the monastery. They had to get back before sundown, but some prayed late into the night and returned to their rooms relying on the faint light of the occasional streetlamp.

"What do you think we'll find if we walk out there?" I asked, pointing at the pitch-dark.

"Houses, a sunflower field, a lavender field, farms, wine shops, restaurants. I heard there's a small stream if you walk farther on and then a lake. And small chapels in between," said Hanji.

"I heard there's other things," I said.

"Like what?"

"Teens having sex inside barns."

Hanji laughed, nodding, then said, "Is that how you talk to the sisters, too?"

We both laughed.

"Let's go and check out what's there. We can go when our shift is over," Hanji said with that innocent look of his.

I shook my head quietly. I said I didn't want to take a night stroll at the risk of endangering myself in an unfamiliar land.

As strolls outside the monastery were not permitted after nine, some visitors lied that they were couples staying in the family lodgings. We pretended to believe them and let them out of the monastery.

Hanji and I talked about a great deal of things sitting on that bench. At times I was so immersed in our conversation that I would only come to my senses when visitors slipping out of the monastery had gotten far away from us. I knew whatever I told him wouldn't get out to the world, and above all I had faith that he would not judge me for what I said. Embarrassing memories, things I couldn't forgive myself for, I could talk about them all in front of Hanji without much self-censorship. I told him stories I can't write about even here—they belong solely to him.

Even so, there were moments that struck me speechless.

Like when Hanji asked me what my home was like, and why so many people committed suicide in such an affluent country. I couldn't give him adequate answers, and was ashamed of my inability to articulate the world I lived in. Instead of answering, I told him about the lives led by my grandma, my mom, the woman who lived next door. Because that seemed to be a more appropriate answer to Hanji's questions.

Hanji told me about himself, too. He mentioned that two and a half million of the three million people living in Nairobi lived in slums, that he grew up without comprehending how his parents could be so unperturbed about such extreme injustice. As he watched his parents go to church and pray only for the well-being of their family, he thought of the children dying mere kilometers away from that church. At the same time, Hanji admitted that his father's money had given him a good education and his mother's devotion to the family had allowed him to lead an untroubled life. He said he shut his eyes whenever he perceived that his privilege was rooted in his parents' wealth, and that their wealth was likely the outcome of exploitation. Even so, he confessed, the only thing he truly believed in and counted on was money.

We checked our watches only when all the couples who had ventured outside the monastery returned and we could no longer hear any laughter or chatter. It was one in the morning. I had checked the time expecting it to be around eleven.

We finished evening prayer and went to the previous day's bench.

"I have something to show you," said Hanji. He took out a small, palm-size album from the sling bag he always carried. We held up the photographs in the album to the light of a streetlamp.

The first one showed about twenty people in a kitchen standing very straight. In the center of the photograph, a woman in a green dress with a yellow floral print cradled a baby wrapped in a white blanket. A turban matching her dress covered her head. Hanji pointed at the bundled baby and said, "That's me. And those people are my closest family."

Everyone in Hanji's family, both women and men, had broad shoulders and large feet. Hanji's mom had the build of a brawny man. To my eyes, Hanji looked like a small puppy in the arms of his mother.

"Who's the little one?" I asked, pointing at a child who looked to be around three and was staring at the camera, clutching his mother's dress.

"My older brother."

"Is he your only sibling?"

"No. I have a younger sister."

Hanji thumbed through the album to show me a picture. A baby, who scarcely looked a hundred days old, was fast asleep in her crib. Hanji turned some more pages and showed me another picture. It was clearly of the same child, now five or maybe six, sleeping. There was one of her in her teens lying on her bed. The teenager had filled out more in her face and neck and sported short hair. Her head rested on a pillow covered with a gauze towel and her mouth was slightly open; she looked serene, as if she were dreaming a good dream.

"Do you have any photos of her where she's not sleeping?"

Hanji showed me a picture of his younger sister smiling, lying down. She was scrunching up her face to smile.

"Leah's always been lying down like this ever since she was born."

Hanji flipped through the album to another photograph. She had put on more weight than in the previous picture, and in front of her stood Hanji, his mom, and his dad, all of whom were smiling.

"We took this one on Leah's birthday," said Hanji, and gazed at her face for a long moment. A warm light flickered in his face.

"She's beautiful, isn't she?"

I nodded at his words.

"Ever since I was a kid, I went to Leah whenever I had too much on my mind. Or when my brother beat me and bullied me behind my parents' back, I sought out Leah's room, where she was asleep, and cried quietly. I'd gaze into her sleeping face and my mind would calm down. Sometimes I imagined what games we might've played if she were like other kids. Leah's mind has stayed at two years old."

I thought of young Hanji sitting in that room, watching Leah. A lifetime of having to look after a family member was beyond me.

Hanji said his mom and dad, brother, grandma, and aunts took turns attending to Leah. But someday he would have to be the main caretaker, so he had known from a young age that his life was not just his own.

"I've never thought about getting married or having a kid or anything like that. I need to be responsible for Leah. I need to earn money, I need to hire someone reliable to take care of her while I'm away."

Hanji's family flipped Leah's body over once every two hours to prevent her from getting bedsores, and at least two people had to work together to bathe her. Hanji's parents, who used to travel at every opportunity, couldn't even go anywhere nearby after Leah was born. That was a very painful experience, Hanji said, but the pain wasn't everything; all of his family loved and adored Leah to bits.

Leah gave her family the gift of silence. They had time to watch sleeping Leah for at least two or three times a day in silence, and those trivial hours gave Hanji strength of mind.

"Sometimes she cries and throws tantrums. It's natural as she's a child. On some days she cries nonstop for hours. And when she does, I've really hated her and hated the situation, I've even wanted to hit her if that was what it took to shut her up. I'm a terrible person."

"Hanji, you're an incredibly good person."

"Youngju . . . you're so simple."

I changed the subject to lighten the suddenly awkward mood.

"Is this your first trip?"

"It is. I've never even really been to the places just outside of Nairobi. Going to the Serengeti National Park for a school field trip was my only time."

"Serengeti?"

"You drive around in a Jeep and watch wild animals."

"That's cool."

"To me, the Serengeti Park was the edge of the world. The park's meadows were so vast you couldn't see where they ended, and in primary school I really thought they never ended. I came back from the field trip gushing about the Serengeti to Mom and Dad, and I still wasn't satisfied so I ran to Leah's room and told her exaggerated stories about the things I saw. I felt bad after telling her. Because I'd gone off to see amazing sights while she lay there, unable to move a single step her whole life."

Hanji said he thought of Leah when he ate good food outside, when he dated a girl, when he danced at a club, when he sang. He said he would be sad for her then, but quieted his heart by thinking that such pity was an arrogance toward Leah.

"To me, Leah isn't a separate person. I'm here talking to you right now, but a part of my body is lying in my Nairobi home. Wherever I go, whatever I do, a part of me is always in Nairobi."

Hanji's gaze lingered on Leah in the photograph even as he said those words. The light flickering in his face fell on my pale heart.

I interlace my fingers with Hanji's.

I kiss his neck.

I fall asleep with him on the bench, under the shade of a tree.

I get on a plane, accompany Hanji to Nairobi, and meet his tall family members I've seen in the photograph. They welcome me and accept me. I follow Hanji into Leah's room and say hello. He looks at me with the same warm eyes he reserves for Leah. He and I recklessly cross Nairobi's roads, which as he said don't have any crosswalks, then we hop on a bus and head to the Serengeti meadows. There, we run into Hanji's rhinos. They look healthy and happy. We watch the sun set on the meadows together with the rhinos.

I bear Hanji's child, and stay in Nairobi where there are no cold winters. We talk about this monastery. We say we can't remember very well, it was too long ago. We say that the time before we had each other was incomplete.

I can't escape Nairobi.

I change Leah's diapers, I prop her head up and feed her soup. My beautiful baby sits crying on the floor and Hanji doesn't come home. I miss the days we first met.

Those two weeks passed, our night guard duty ending with them. But Hanji and I continued to meet at the mouth of that road after evening prayer, as if by unspoken agreement. While we couldn't have long conversations like before, we chatted briefly to check what the other had done all day.

It was hard to make out Hanji in places beyond the reach of streetlamps. His body mixed in with the darkness. His eyes were all I saw clearly, but I could tell what he was thinking, what he was feeling, just by looking at them.

Hanji's face stiffened at times.

It was not the naturally relaxed face I had seen the first time I met him. For the briefest moment, he would look like a dead man. The face of someone who didn't exist here. I thought in such moments that he must be in Nairobi by Leah's side.

Words no longer spilled out of us. Now for some seconds, now for some minutes, we walked without a word to each other, picking up slugs that had crawled out to the road and throwing them back into the tall grass. In the silence, I realized how much I was clinging to this moment. This moment had to go on forever. It could not be allowed to slip away carelessly like the other moments dumped and scrapped into the past.

We often went outside the monastery for a stroll.

Just beyond the front gates was a graveyard where brothers were laid to rest. The flowers planted in every corner of the graveyard made it look like a small flower garden. Names were written on plain wooden crosses, years of birth and death recorded on tombstones. The grave of the brother who founded the monastery was there, a softhearted man who moved to this small village where he didn't know a soul, just because of that one remark by an old woman: "Thank you for coming to this desolate place." We stood still in front of his grave and watched his wooden cross in silence as if by tacit agreement.

The graveyard overlooked a hill, on which stood a tall lime tree. When the wind blew, the tree's long, tender branches brushed our faces as we walked beneath it and the fragrance of its flowers, mingled with the smell of freshly cut grass from the field, tickled our noses. At the foot of the hill lived a horse we named Peter, to whom we fed the apples and biscuits saved from our last meal. When we sliced the apples into quarters with a pocketknife and placed them on our palms, Peter's thick tongue would lick our palms and snatch up the apples. When we called out "Peter," he would amble toward us even if he was far away, his hooves falling heavily on the ground. As he drew nearer, we would see the swarm of flies gathered in the corners of his bloodshot eyes.

Past Peter, a wide meadow stretched to the south. We would take a path across the meadow while watching short-furred sheep napping in the shade of trees. Walking eastward from the meadow, we would come upon a small Catholic church built of stone. Black birds gathered on the roof of the church, their wings tucked in. We normally turned back to the monastery at that point but walked farther on if time permitted. A village started from there. The two-story houses were mostly old, but the colorful flowers abloom on their walls and balconies imbued them with a bright warmth.

Once past the village, a small stream running under a concrete bridge came into view. We liked to take our shoes off and sit still, dipping our feet in the water.

Not everything we encountered there was good.

Some people called me "Chinese" from above the bridge, and the more aggressive ones shrieked "Fuck off, you immigrants!" and pretended to throw the alcohol bottle they were drinking from. We stared blankly up at the bridge on such occasions— because we weren't afraid in the slightest. Some people swore in

French so I asked Hanji what they were saying, but he smiled and said it was nothing.

I sat there motionless, thinking about the people who spat out racist remarks at us and ran off. What sort of people were they? Where were they headed after crossing the bridge? Probably the grocery store, then home, or the bar to meet friends. They, too, must be someone's dear friend or family, and at times they must also feel insulted by their clients or bosses. They, too, must remember being discriminated against due to their looks, age, background, or someone's prejudice, and must have experienced rejection by someone they loved.

Did they want revenge?

Or did they just want to provoke you to see how you'd react? Truly, I pitied these people who couldn't feel secure about themselves in any other way. How empty a life of deriving joy from mocking and discriminating against another was.

Time moved quickly there, and I constantly checked my watch because I was sorry for every moment passed. I felt we had barely exchanged a few words, yet thirty to forty minutes had gone by and it was already time to go back. We toweled off our wet feet and walked back to the monastery at a slightly brisk pace. I had to almost jog to keep up with Hanji.

Every Monday there was a gathering for the volunteers leaving the monastery. It was held in a lounge perhaps no bigger than a hundred fifty square feet. We placed a table before the departing volunteers, lit a few candles, and listened to them speak about their experience. Colleagues who had been close to them reminisced about the times spent together, and those who played instruments or sang well gave performances. Cynthia from Mexico performed a one-woman show while Gustavo from Colombia did a mime. We played games if time permitted.

In that small room, thirty volunteers with different nationalities huddled together. No one's mother tongue was English. We spoke in English and added "Can you understand me?" like a refrain to a song. To someone whose first language was English, we probably would've sounded like ten-year-olds. Nevertheless, we did everything to try to understand each other, whether through poor English or interpreting done in poor English. It was hard to imagine how everyone who spoke in halting English would sound in their mother tongues.

The mood of that gathering belonged solely to that gathering.

No single culture dominated, and none could anyway. People voluntarily sang, strummed the guitar, acted, and mimed while not being great at any of these things. There was no obvious common topic we could discuss. Apart from a few people, we knew absolutely nothing about each other. We didn't know how old anyone was, what kind of education they had received, where they lived, what their political leanings were, or why they were here. Still, we tried our best to make sense of each other's awkward utterances, sentence by sentence, sitting in two circles in that narrow space. We sat like that as if sitting in circles was the only purpose of our gathering.

Latin Americans who couldn't speak English at all attended the gathering and listened to the interpreting by others who spoke Spanish and English, while Africans who spoke only French listened to the interpreting by those who spoke French and English. Whenever someone said something, it was interpreted across the room simultaneously. A very short sentence in English followed by a long interpretation prompted people who didn't speak the language to burst into laughter.

In a way, all the volunteers from Africa reminded me of Hanji. They laughed a lot and moved their bodies freely. They laughed as if a law forbade them from missing the slightest opportunity for laughter. Watching Hanji laugh and talk among them, I thought maybe he felt bored and uncomfortable around me.

Hanji interpreted into French for the African volunteers sitting by the window. He told what must be simple facts as though they were entertaining tales, assuming so many expressions and punctuating his delivery with roars of laughter. Everyone conversing with Hanji looked highly amused. Even the people who rarely smiled beamed in his presence. Hanji around other people struck me as a different person from the Hanji I knew when he and I were alone.

In those moments, Hanji was further away from me than ever before.

I didn't know Hanji. I didn't know his world, the world that grew a little warmer and brighter whenever he touched it.

I was lying on the sofa in the dormitory common room when Caro plopped down next to me. Her chocolate skin glimmered and her small face was beautiful, as if someone had molded it with the utmost care. Eyes with large, sparkling black pupils. She looked intently at me with those eyes for a moment then began, "I saw you talking to Hanji yesterday. You were talking on the road to the village, after the farewell gathering, right?"

"Right."

"You guys kept picking stuff up from the ground and throwing them. What were they?"

"Slugs."

Caro made a face and laughed.

"Youngju. Hanji's such a dork. He's really special."

How much did Caro know about Hanji? Had he told the things he'd shared with me to everyone he knew? I became curious.

"You seem a lot different from my first impression of you," said Caro.

"What was your first impression of me?"

"I thought you were a nun. A really conservative one. I'm not joking." Then, evidently worried I might be offended, she quickly added, "It was biased of me to think that. You turned out to be as big of a dork as Hanji. I heard so much about you from Hanji. He said you were his closest friend here. I've known him over three years, but I've never seen him this close to someone."

"Hanji?"

"Yes."

"But Hanji seems to get along with everyone."

"He gets along with everyone, but you can never tell what he's thinking. I haven't seen him express dislike to a single soul. Probably because he doesn't want to hurt them. Everyone resents him a little, though. He's endlessly nice to them, but that's it. Maybe I should say they're disappointed instead? Sometimes he seems to connect with animals better than with people."

I quietly watched Caro's beautiful face say those words. Her well-proportioned features and round head, her glimmering skin I wanted to touch. A girl as beautiful as you, I thought, wouldn't throw slugs into the tall grass with Hanji.

"I actually don't know Hanji that well, either," I said. "I'm not sure why he said he's closest to me. You know we don't have enough time to talk to each other because there's too much work here."

I might've been honest with her if I had liked Hanji a little less.

Truth is, Caro, Hanji and I talk every day. We stroll around the monastery when neither of us have shifts, then at night we get a bottle of Coke from the store's vending machine and share it. Past midnight, we sometimes sit still under the tree by the water fountain. How should I put this. If I were allowed to say this . . . Hanji knows me. And I imagine his mind, as he had imagined the rhinos' minds. Sometimes I sit on the balcony of his house, though I've never been there.

Hanji may have casually mentioned he was close to me, but I can't say that about him. Because if I said one word about Hanji, I feel like everyone would see through me to my fantasies about him. I'm a little crazy in that sense.

"Youngju, how old are you, by the way?"

I hesitated at Caro's question.

Every time I bumped into Hanji, the skin on my back and my abdomen prickled and I could hear the blood rush to my head. My heart pounded loudly and I kept stammering. A fire spread from my calves to the back of my neck at the thought of Hanji looking at me from afar.

I pictured the geologic timescale in my head when that happened.

In grade seven, I was gifted a geologic timescale, which I stuck to the wall and liked to read from beginning to end. In order of era, I memorized the names of organisms that had lived in each until I could recite the whole scale by the time I started high school. I did it because the names of things that weren't here now but had once clearly existed felt precious.

The proto-Earth.

There was no life on the proto-Earth. I imagined a blackboard with nothing drawn on it.

The Archean Eon.

Bacteria, cyanobacteria, and archaea appeared. Tiny dots drawn by the tip of white chalk.

The Proterozoic Eon.

Jellyfish appeared. Gossamer jellyfish whose bodies you could see through.

The Cambrian Period.

Shellfish, corals, trilobites.

The Ordovician Period.

Starfish and creatures called sea scorpions. The vanished conodonts.

The Silurian Period.

Snails, clams, mussels. Jawless fish.

I could recite the names of these creatures as you would a prayer. Jawed fish, lungfish, land snails, sea lilies, reptile-like mammals, cycads, archaeopteryxes, the first flowering plants. When I repeated these names in my head, I lost interest in the outside world, the thoughts and feelings in me dulled, and my existence seemed to fade a little.

Time and place no longer mattered.

When I was sad, anxious, or angry, when someone seized my heart and shook it, I desperately called out those names, and to some extent they did separate me from suffering. Once I muttered everything from "the proto-Earth" to "various hoofed mammals," it seemed that I wasn't the one calling their names, but they mine. I wasn't alone in that stretch of time.

Did Hanji know? That I had been silently uttering the names of vanished organisms beside him. That I had tried to repress my feelings for him by doing so. That above all, I was scared he might read my thoughts. That I had resolved to run far away if he so much as had an inkling of my feelings.

I had no presence wherever I was. Hanji stood out in every crowd.

I had no confidence and mumbled my words. Hanji spoke naturally in any company.

I covered my mouth because I couldn't even smile properly. Hanji's expressions were genuine.

Maybe it wasn't that Hanji liked me, but simply thought of me as a misfit whom he needed to take under his wing.

We were not equals. That was why we couldn't be lovers. I wasn't even good enough to be his friend. No one told me that and they probably didn't think so, either, but I myself was keenly aware of it. Brooding about these things made me think of my ex-boyfriend, who used to say I was "letting" him date me. What had bound us together for three long years might have been our shared sense of self-degradation. Only, his inferiority complex was worse than mine, which had allowed me to despise him and avoid despising myself.

"**What are you thinking** about?" Hanji asked.

"I'm thinking about how you'll be returning to Nairobi in a month and a half."

Hanji said nothing.

"How much of our time here do you think we'll remember when we go back to our normal lives?" I asked.

"We'll probably forget most of it," Hanji replied.

"I hate that."

"Hate what?"

"Forgetting."

I took out a notebook from my bag and opened it for him to see. "This is my diary. I've been writing in it every day since I arrived. You can read it."

He turned a page over, then the next, and laughed out loud. "The letters look like some kind of drawing. Look," he said as he pointed at one of the characters I had written: 夭. "This one looks like a person dancing."

Hanji touched the characters as if he found them fascinating.

"Oh, this I can read. June twenty-third. That's the day I got here," he said. "I was tired from driving an old car all the way to Lyon Airport, on a hot day at that. This Hanji guy from Nairobi, or whatever his name was, kept talking in French and was so loud I wanted to hit him. And why on earth would he talk to me when I was dozing off in the church? He forgot to bring his toothbrush when he'll be away from home for three months? Thanks to him, I had to take him to the store." Hanji was making up a story while tracing his fingers over the text as if he could read Hangul, and we had a laugh.

"Did you write about me in here at all?" Hanji asked.

Ever since June twenty-third, you appear in it every single day.

"You're not in it very much," I said jokingly.

"Hey, I thought you were my friend." Hanji grinned.

I pointed at the letters 한지 in the sentence "Hanji is working at the big kitchen" and said, "That's your name."

Hanji gazed quietly down at the letters. I wrote 한지 again in the notebook in large print and showed it to him.

"It's beautiful," he said. "What does your name look like?"

I wrote 영주 beside 한지. The letters 한지 and 영주 looked affectionate together.

"You sure won't forget your time here," Hanji said as he flipped through my notebook. "I find it hard to write. How do you record things every day like this? You have to tell me about our time here when we meet up later. I forget easily."

"I will, definitely."

In this manner, we always assumed we would meet again despite knowing it would be difficult. We talked as if we would meet again like next-door neighbors a doorbell-press away, as if we lived close enough to pop over to each other's houses in our slippers when one invited the other to dinner, and by doing so we tried to ignore the fact that we would likely have nothing to do with each other for the rest of our lives.

"Youngju. I know. That we will meet again," said Hanji.

"Yeah."

I gazed at 한지 and 영주 sitting side by side in my notebook.

한지 **and** 영주 are still in my notebook.

When I read through my records of that time, I can feel the laughs and stories we had shared, the nightscapes, and even the scent of lime tree blossoms mingled in the evening air. Everything is vivid: Hanji's face when he smiled at me, the thin-soled slippers he had bought from the store, the Coke we had shared, and the crude bench that kept falling backward because one of its legs was shaky. And yet those stories are losing their light as if they never happened. Though I remember the details of my time with Hanji, their reality continues to fade.

I still don't know why Hanji turned his back on me.

I don't understand that rupture.

I tell myself to let go of what I can't understand even with the passing of time, yet I am incapable of properly forgetting a single small memory.

At first I thought Hanji hadn't seen me. There was no way he could've seen me smile and wave then pretend he hadn't. But he passed me again and again that day without acknowledging me, and didn't show up at the bench where we met every night, either. I thought maybe he was sick. That is, until I saw him on my way back to the dormitory from the bench, hanging out and laughing with the other African volunteers. I raised my hand again and waved, but Hanji looked away.

This happened two weeks before Hanji left for Nairobi, on September 12.

I wrote, *Hanji looked away.*

We had sat on that bench and talked even on the night before Hanji looked away from me. We hadn't argued, nor had something happened that might have hurt each other's feelings. We had just discussed our day as usual. I remember mentioning that I cleaned the dormitory just vacated by a group of visitors who had stayed there a week. I told him it had been tough removing the sheets from the mattresses, gathering them up, and carrying them to the laundry room. Hanji said the monastery looked a little lonely, now that there were fewer people than when he first came. That was it.

Maybe he was upset from something I couldn't remember. Maybe I had made a rude joke. But I had always been careful as I didn't want to hurt someone I liked. I wasn't a child who spoke as I pleased without realizing what I was saying. Even if I had upset or offended him, couldn't we have talked it out? Had I committed something so serious that he couldn't look me in the face and talk? Or had somebody spoken ill of me or tried to drive us apart? If someone slandered you, I thought, I would not have believed them and would've at least checked with you.

Hanji had said "See you tomorrow" that night, too. In the dark, with those affectionate eyes, you had said that to me.

Something did trouble me, though. Hanji occasionally said I was "simple." He always said it laughingly, but there were a few times when I somehow felt he meant it. Once, after saying "You're so simple," he added, as if to explain himself, "Simplicity is good."

I still don't know what he meant by my simplicity.

"Memory is a talent. You were born with it," my grandma told me when I was young. "But it's a painful one. So, try to make yourself a little less sensitive. Be extra cautious with happy memories, my dear. Happy memories seem like jewels when in fact they're burning charcoal. You'll hurt yourself if you hold on to them, so let go and dust off your hands. Child, they are no gift."

But I remember.

My grandma, who was a Buddhist, said people reincarnate because of their memory of this life. Once your heart stuck to a memory, she said, you couldn't wrench it off, and so you were born again and again. She told me not to suffer too much when a loved one dies or leaves, that I should mourn as much as I needed to without getting swallowed up by my sadness. Or else I would keep coming back into this world. That last part scared me.

Time passes, people leave, we become alone again.

If we don't accept that fact, memory erodes the present and exhausts the mind until it ages us and ails us.

That is what Grandma told me.

I remember those words always.

Hanji began to openly treat me like an invisible person.

Not only did he ignore my greetings but also doubled back if he ran into me. His eyes didn't contain a modicum of rage. They just looked indifferent, faint, tired. I couldn't chase after him or even call his name. I didn't have the guts.

I watched Hanji clean up garbage from a distance. He wore an elbow-length glove on his right hand and held a pair of tongs with his left. He pulled out plastic bottles, glass bottles, and paper boxes from the garbage bin and put them in a mesh bag, repeating those steps. Beads of sweat dropped from his chin, and his neck, armpits, and the back of his blue T-shirt were soaked. Mouth slightly open and bent over, he concentrated on the task in silence.

I had expected to lose Hanji someday, but not now.

When Hanji smiled at me, made time for me to walk with me, said he considered me his closest friend, I had thought his attentions were undeserved. But it was still unfair to end all of that without any explanation.

I approached Hanji while he cleaned the garbage. I felt faint.

"Hanji."

He looked at me mutely, his face stiff and devoid of any kind of smile. The instant I saw that face I forgot what I had wanted to say and was struck speechless. Hanji's gaze lingered on my face for a moment, then it left me.

The mesh bag Hanji held in one hand was full of plastic bottles. I noticed a few flies sitting on Coke bottles that looked extremely sticky and heard people shrieking with laughter somewhere. While I struggled to say something, Hanji gathered up the mouth of the bag, gripped it in one hand, and stalked away, rigid as a wooden doll.

I stood still before the garbage bin and stared at the spot Hanji had occupied just moments before. Hanji had not said a thing to me, but I knew. Why he was avoiding me wasn't important. He was avoiding me now, and refusing to accept that would be the same as harassing him.

I did not want to harass him.

It would be wrong of me to apologize in any way or press him for an explanation.

People leave. That was what my grandma used to say.

I just have to accept that fact as it is, I whispered to myself.

Sometimes I have a dream. It's a dream about taking a night-time stroll.

As on the proto-Earth, there is no life in the world. No slugs, no lime trees, no flies, no Peter swarming with flies, no napping sheep, no Hanji's rhinos, no young people or old, no grad students, no monks, no racists or the garbage they pour out.

In that empty darkness I think, *What a lonesome place Earth once was.*

Earth, I realize, has simply been uplifting and eroding itself, depositing itself tirelessly.

How tireless, how lonesome.

The world is ashen and a volcano rumbles from afar. I head toward it. I walk for a long time until I see the chapel near the monastery, the family lodgings, the village I strolled through with Hanji. I catch sight of Hanji and me in the distance dipping their feet in the stream. The two of them are all that exists in the world. I have to get down from the bridge and reach them, fast, but I can't find a way down. No amount of struggle brings me down from the bridge.

The scene changes abruptly.

Hanji and I are sitting on the bench by the water fountain. We sit still in the dark.

Hanji says, "We will meet again. When we do, tell me about the memories I lost. Because I'll forget everything, including you, this moment."

Hanji smiles sadly as he says that.

I want to reply, but my mouth won't open. I strain myself to look at Hanji, only to find in his place a large mesh bag with its jaws gaping. The mesh bag full of plastic bottles Hanji shoved into it.

I didn't want to stage a protest about my pain to other people.

I simply did my share of the work, I ate, and I attended communal prayers three times a day. In the time I used to spend walking with Hanji, I read at the dormitory common room or drank hot chocolate and chatted with the other volunteers. At night I played card games, made yarn bracelets with the Latin girls, or played quasi Ping-Pong. I laughed till I had tears in my eyes. My roommates were all asleep by the time I returned to my room around midnight. I crawled under my blankets and soundlessly cried myself to sleep.

Caro came to see me on one of those nights. She opened the door to my room and whispered my name. "Youngju."

I pulled my blanket over my head and pretended to sleep.

"Wake up, Youngju. It won't take long."

I rubbed my tear-stained face against my pillow and got up. We walked to the front of the warehouse and spread paper boxes on the ground to sit.

"Sorry to wake you up. But I couldn't find a way to talk to you otherwise. I noticed you were always with other people in the common room except when you worked."

"I was."

"I got the feeling you were avoiding talking to me one-on-one."

"I never avoided you."

"Alright then, my bad. You probably know what I'm going to talk to you about."

I said nothing.

"It's about Hanji. Has something happened between you and him?" Caro's voice shook ever so slightly.

Caro's beautiful face. You don't know a thing. Suddenly, I found myself angry at her, though she had done nothing wrong.

"Why are *you* asking me that?"

"Just curious. Why you two don't even say hi when you used to be glued to each other. Everyone talks about it, you know, though they don't mention it in front of you two. Hanji looks tired. He didn't come to the African social this Tuesday, and apparently he doesn't really hang out with people back in the dorm, either."

"So what?"

"I don't know why you're treating Hanji like that. He's a good person, you know."

Words failed me.

"I don't know what you heard from Hanji," I said.

"He hasn't said anything."

"Then why are you making all these assumptions and concluding I'm the one at fault, then pull me out of bed so late to harass me?"

I sensed I was saying horrible things. Caro was simply asking out of concern for Hanji, but I was reacting emotionally. A part of me detached from myself observed my emotional outburst in indifference.

"You talk and laugh," said Caro. "You play card games and Ping-Pong with the others. Meanwhile, Hanji suffers." Although her tone was cautious, in her words I heard a voice that judged me.

"Yes. I do. But what's it to you?" I said bluntly in my rudimentary English, petty and sharp as the words spat out by a child. I wanted to explain how Hanji was ignoring me, how much that pained me, and why, nonetheless, I couldn't ask him why he was doing this to me—but I couldn't do it. The English words floating in my head failed to form order and got tangled and could not be said out loud. Caro. That's not what I wanted to say. Give me a moment. A moment to think, choose the right words, and make a sentence.

Caro looked at me with her large eyes. My blunt words couldn't hurt Caro. What I saw in her eyes was disappointment. Eyes that said, So this is all you are.

"I said what I said because I was just worried about you two. I've told you this before, but Hanji has never been so close to someone as he's been with you. Youngju, Hanji is a good person. I was relieved to see him finally make a good friend. Because he's always had this invisible wall up. I thought he'd managed to break it down here, but he looks hurt."

I was silent for a moment then said, "Hanji is avoiding me. I can't even talk to him."

"Did you fight?"

"No. We talked on the day before he started avoiding me."

"Really?"

"Yes."

"Youngju. I don't understand you. Then just go and confront him. Ask why he's avoiding you. You have to talk it out. Pretending nothing's wrong like you're doing now isn't good for you or Hanji. You're lying to yourself by acting cheerful here when you have an unresolved issue on your mind."

"I'm going to bed now. I have a morning shift," I said as if I hadn't heard her.

Caro. I don't want to harass Hanji.

I worked in the diet kitchen that week. Some of the visitors were lactose or gluten intolerant or had allergies to beans, nuts, meats, shrimp, tomatoes, and such. The diet kitchen cooked exclusively for them. We boiled potatoes and carrots and eggs there, cooked rice, steamed couscous, and washed lettuce to use in salads. A few people could eat cheese, so we brought some out in a basket.

We were out of cheese that day and the person in charge of the diet kitchen sent me to the big kitchen. I knew Hanji was working there, but the big kitchen was spacious enough that he wouldn't see me from the cooking station if I popped into the refrigerated pantry behind it and came back out.

I switched on the pantry's light and walked in to find Hanji holding a box of apples.

I looked at his face for a second, then stepped aside for him without a word. But he just stood there, watching me with the apple box in his arms.

I put single-serve cream cheese packets into my basket. When I finished filling the basket with cheese and turned around, Hanji was still standing at the same spot. The round light affixed to the pantry ceiling blinked. Even as Hanji looked at me like he wanted to say something, he didn't say a word.

The mere fact that he hadn't avoided me was a relief and gave me the courage to speak to him.

Dropping my gaze to the apples in the box he held, I said, "Thank you for not avoiding me. I won't take too much of your time. We can't stay long anyway since it's freezing here. So please hear me out. Don't leave like I'm not here," I finished, and looked up at Hanji's face.

He was crying.

"I won't ask you why you've been acting this way. It would feel good to know, but what's the point. If I did something wrong to you, whether you forgive me or not is your choice. If you're doing this not because of something I did but for your own reasons, I can understand them whatever they are. But if you've misunderstood me because of what someone said, and if you couldn't see my sincerity, it really is a shame." As I spoke, I shook from both the cold and fear. "I don't care how badly you treat me. There's no way in the world I could hate you. I'm fine meeting like this, I just want to stay in the same space as you. When I think about how I won't see you here in a week, I tear up even while I walk. I guess I won't be able to talk to you like this anymore. Hanji, please don't walk out of my life like this."

I fought back tears and tried my best to talk calmly. "Hanji. I won't bother you anymore. Take care in Nairobi. You said you easily forget what happened in the past, so leave just the good memories and forget the rest. No, forget the good memories, too. I hope you'll always be healthy, Hanji. And that your family, and Leah, will be, too."

"Hanji! You in there?"

Someone knocked on the door from the outside, looking for him.

Hanji wiped away his tears with the back of his hand and walked out of the pantry.

I went out soon, too, but the chill that had seeped into my bones was slow to dissipate. My forehead alone burned hot.

I requested silent meditation for a week.

I gathered up all my belongings at the dorm and went to the Silence House, which was situated outside the monastery. It was an old, two-story house with a large garden. I say "garden," but it was a chaotic bed of untended plants that looked fit for a snake to crawl out from at night. In the Silence House, you had a room to yourself and every meal was delivered to you from the monastery. You walked half an hour to the monastery for communal prayers and were exempted from labor for the week.

A day without labor was long and painful. I tried to pull myself together and read, but my eyes registered none of the words, while my anxieties and delusions, hitherto suppressed by the fatigue of labor, began to rein free inside me. The most pathetic of my thoughts was the delusion that I might still be on good terms with Hanji if I'd done this or that in the past.

When he asked me to take a stroll in the middle of the night, what if I had joined him instead of refusing? When he asked if he was in my notebook, what if I'd just been honest with him, and told him most of the stuff I wrote was about him? When he talked about the animals he couldn't save, what if I hadn't stayed silent from surprise and instead said, That's not your fault, to comfort him? In the time I spent babbling on about the origin of slugs, what if I had given him the chance to say what he wanted to say to me? Had that simplicity of mine suffocated him? Perhaps I had tried to see him too often. Had I monopolized the time he wanted to himself and driven him to get sick of me?

Silence forced me to see my naked desires frankly.

The desire to be loved, the desire to connect with someone deeply and inseparably, the desire to forget, to *not* forget, the desire to be understood completely without being dissected, the desire to avoid getting hurt, the desire to love even if I did get hurt, and above all, the desire to see Hanji.

After meeting him in the refrigerated pantry, I tried not to see Hanji.

I could've seen him if I sat in the volunteer seating area of the church or went to the big kitchen, but I made a conscious effort to steer clear of him. He was due to return to Nairobi in less than a week now, and I thought imagining he was already gone would be the less painful option; choosing not to see him now was better than being unable to see him later.

Whenever Hanji entered my thoughts, I paced through the tall grass of the garden reciting the geologic timescale. But my recitations could not stop me from thinking about him. Hanji breathed in every geologic era. He was there when the Earth was first formed, when the planet didn't have a hard surface, when land animals hadn't yet appeared. He would live on in eternity for as long as I remember. I accepted this fact.

I sat on a chair placed in a corner of the garden and wrote what I wanted to say to Hanji. I wrote in Korean first, then in English. English with terrible spelling and articles missing here and there.

Hanji,

I am at the Silence House now. It's five in the afternoon and the weather is a little chilly.

Tonight, you will have a farewell gathering with the others. Someone will play the guitar and sing, someone will

reminisce about the time they spent with you. You and
Caro will talk about your stay here and thank everyone. I
won't be there and you will be relieved that I haven't
showed up.

Tomorrow you will leave for Nairobi, and be reunited
with your family in your home by evening. How glad Leah
will be to see you. And how happy you will be to see her.
You will take a shower, unpack, and eat with your family.
You will show them the pictures on your phone and talk
about this place as if only good things have happened here.
All the while feeling inwardly sorry that your family can't
go anywhere. So you will become more dedicated to your
family, and soon resume working at the animal hospital.

You will become a little confused once time passes. It will
feel strange that there was a time when you stayed at a
monastery in a remote French village, that you shared your
story to a small Korean girl and met her every day for a
stroll. The reason you ignored my greetings and turned
your back on me will have faded by then. When you think
of me again then, I will have turned into a faceless,
voiceless person already. I will have become someone who
left the faintest trace in your life, or perhaps no trace at all,
a stranger whose life has nothing to do with yours.

Like you, I will also leave this place someday and go
back to where I used to live. I will start commuting to the

school lab again, deal with rocks, go on research trips to the caves of Japan and China. I will put on more age-appropriate clothes and expressions, strive not to create conflicts with anyone, and very occasionally recall my time here. The time when I was most able to be myself. I will remember you and me from that time.

Thank you for keeping me company in my desolate heart.

Hanji,

I hope that the time you have ahead of you will be full of blessing.

I wish you the blessing of oblivion, and that you will find the strength to exist moment by moment.

Youngju

I wrote that, tore off the page containing my English translation of the Korean, and chucked it. I walked back to the monastery with the notebook in my bag, the notebook where I had recorded every single day of my seven months there in Korean.

It was evening prayer time. There was song and silence, followed by more song, then the brothers filed out of the church.

Hanji sat still in the volunteer seating area, gazing at an icon attached to one of the church pillars. How long he sat like that, I don't know. He stood up and walked to the front of the church and leaned against the wall, closing his eyes. That was the last image I would see of Hanji. I couldn't approach him.

People leave.

I got up and walked out of the church. Caro was standing outside.

"Take care, Caro," I whispered in her ear.

"You don't have to talk. You're doing silent meditation," she said. I handed her a postcard I had written. It was about how thankful I was for the last three months and, though I never got to tell her in person, what a beautiful person she was. She handed me a postcard, too. I put it in my bag and said goodbye to her for the last time.

On my way back to the Silence House, I met Theo, who had just finished delivering food there. I hesitated a little before I took my notebook out of my bag and held it out to him.

"Please give this to Hanji. It belongs to him."

Theo hesitated a little, too, then took the notebook from me.

"Do you know why Hanji is avoiding me?" I asked.

Theo shook his head. He looked at me as if I were insane.

"I'll give this to him when I see him. He leaves for Nairobi tomorrow."

"I know."

"Aren't you coming to the farewell party later?"

"I'm not going there."

Theo said tentatively, "I'm not sure if I should say this, but the fact that you two never made up till the end is . . . terrible."

Theo always used the word "terrible" to describe negative emotions. He wasn't fluent in English and knew only a handful of adjectives. Unpalatable food, extremely rainy weather, his pimples and curly hair, they were all "terrible" to him. When he called my relationship with Hanji "terrible," the word became an arrow that pierced my consciousness.

This sort of ending to a relationship could not be glossed over with pretty words.

Slowly, I returned to the Silence House.

It was Hanji's last night at the monastery. I stayed up all night, then set out for the monastery in the dark. The flight was at 7:30 a.m. We'll probably leave at five, I remembered Caro saying and walked over, but their car had already gone. I didn't know it then, but I couldn't work up my courage till the very end. I told myself that missing the car was out of my control, but my innermost heart would have known that wasn't true.

I returned to the dormitory two days after Hanji's departure. I had worn summer clothes when I moved into the Silence House, but in one week the temperature had dropped so much that everyone was wearing hoodies or cardigans. One by one without my knowing, the volunteers invited from developing nations had gone back home, leaving only European volunteers and the ones from Colombia and Paraguay. There had been as many as fifty-five volunteers at one point, but that number had shrunk to fifteen within a matter of three weeks. The ever-boisterous common room had become forlorn, with only knitting needles and yarn rolling around the floor once occupied by knitting volunteers. Some people couldn't accept the change and sniffled back tears while they sipped tea.

Their tears held a sweet fondness for those who left. The rare joy, as an adult, of having liked people and lived among them in unconditional friendship. The joy of existing together in that time, a time that could neither last nor be repeated. Their tears grieved for a time devoid of loneliness.

Then the notebook came back to me.

"Hanji didn't take the notebook. He said it was important to you," said Theo. "I didn't mean to read it on purpose, but I opened it by accident, and everything was written in characters I couldn't read. Is this the Korean alphabet?"

"Yes."

"Could Hanji read this?"

"No."

Theo's face was inscrutable as he handed me the notebook.

Theo also left the monastery two days later. I still remember his voice, his strong French accent. Theo had said it was terrible that Hanji and I never made up. As if we had done something awful to each other. I remember how, as he said those words, his face had cringed.

⌒

I roll up the notebook, place it in the hole I have chipped into the ice, and push it deep inside. It slides down without protest, plummeting into the ice. It will not decompose for at least ten thousand years. I don't want to be born again and again over that span of time. Let those memories leave me and latch on to the ice.

Leah's face.

The words: It's okay.

The outline of a body dissolving into the darkness, the occasionally blinking eyes.

The silent eyes and mouth.

The unnatural movement with which he looked away from me.

My simplicity, keeping me from understanding him to the end.

Time flowing above it.

Rupture.

All of it plummets into the ice.

Just like the many lives that had once stayed here and left.

Like Robert Scott, like the conodont, like the saber-toothed cat, like the Ardipithecus.

Desolate, ever desolate.

A Song from Afar

A note on Korean honorifics

Sunbae: used to address someone who joined your school or organization earlier than you did

Hyung: typically used by males to address older males

Oppa: typically used by females to address older males

Unni: typically used by females to address older females

After finishing my spring term lectures I came to St. Petersburg, a decade after Meejin Sunbae began her graduate studies at St. Petersburg University.

I had sent Julia a Facebook message the day before my departure: if she saw an Asian woman in a green maxidress, that was me. *Everybody would look the same to me, to be honest. Could you please find me instead?* I had requested. As I was anxiously wandering around the arrivals gate, Julia put a hand on my shoulder and smiled at me. The very same Polish woman who gazed unsmilingly at the camera next to Meejin Sunbae in every picture the latter had sent. Julia's face had seemed quite cold owing to her dark straight eyebrows, gray eyes, and thin lips, but seeing her smile in person put me at ease.

I had told Julia that I could find my own way to her house if she just told me her address, but she wouldn't hear of it. *I'm coming because I want to. Soeun, you are a precious guest. Please let me come,* she had insisted, and here she was to pick me up.

"Meejin's research office is about a twenty-minute bus ride from my place. The Summer Garden, which she often goes to, is within walking distance, too. I will tell you where her favorite Vietnamese restaurant is." Although Julia's English wasn't perfect, she spoke slowly with an easy-to-understand pronunciation.

"How long did you live with her again?"

"About three years. Meejin was the first roommate I found after moving into this place. We lived together until she moved into her on-campus apartment."

Julia's apartment building was shaped like the character "ㅁ." The Korean equivalent would be a "corridor-style" apartment, except this one had a large open space down its center like a doughnut, which contained a garden. Julia's house was on the third floor, a small space of two bedrooms and a bathroom, living room, laundry room, and kitchen. Julia removed her shoes and placed them by the front door.

"I take off my shoes in the house ever since I lived with Meejin. It's more comfortable that way once you get used to it."

The wooden floor touching my feet felt smooth and cold.

"This was Meejin's room."

I caught a subtle scent of cinnamon when Julia opened the door. There was a single bed, a large oak desk, an empty bookshelf, a three-tier cupboard, a wardrobe, and a large window through which the late evening sunlight slanted in.

"I haven't taken roommates for some time. This room will also be glad to have company. Please let me know if you need anything at any time. This is Soeun's house now."

After a warm shower, I lay down on the bed Meejin Sunbae must have used for three years and pulled the blanket over me. Quietly, I stared at the walls and ceiling through Meejin Sunbae's gaze. Contrary to my expectations, sleep came swiftly, and by the time I opened my eyes it was already ten a.m. Whether it was the six-hour layover in Moscow Airport or the deprivation of sleep from marking exam papers right up to the night before I left, my sleep had been so sound that I hadn't even heard Julia go out. In the kitchen there was toast, an apple, a boiled egg, and orange marmalade on the table.

There is milk and juice in the fridge. There is strong coffee in the coffeemaker. Good day!

Julia had starred my current location on a map of the city and

marked various places with dots and accompanying notes. Meejin's research office, Meejin's apartment, the Vietnamese restaurant, the Summer Garden, the Orthodox cathedral . . . She even
wrote down beside the dots which bus I should take to get there.

Meejin Sunbae was wearing a sky-blue linen sundress. It wasn't a
loose dress, but her small frame made it look like a sack she had
pulled over herself. She held a thin cigarette in one hand as she
studied the menu thoughtfully. Her short, fine hair sparkled in
the sunlight.

"I'm getting vanilla ice cream. You?" I said I would have the
same, so Sunbae called over a server and ordered in Russian. We
chatted about the weather in Seoul and St. Petersburg and each
other's work while we enjoyed our ice creams.

"What took you so long to come? You made it sound like you'd
visit soon."

"I'm sorry."

"Don't be sorry, I feel bad when you apologize so readily."

"I'm apologizing because I really feel sorry."

"Hey, I'm just happy you're here to see me now." The shadow
of a tree dappled her face as she spoke. She looked more at ease
in that moment than I had ever seen her.

"Sitting here with you reminds me of that wall around Marronnier Park," I said. "There was a tree next to it, remember?

And it was thanks to that tree we performed in the summer sitting in the cool shade." A soft smile spread across Sunbae's face at my words. When we first met, she was twenty-five, several years my senior in a student-activist band I joined in college.

We performed at Marronnier Park on Friday evenings in the last week of every month. We sang only with our voices, without microphones or speakers. The low wall around the park was our stage. We climbed to the top of the wall and sang arm in arm, or sometimes hand in hand, swinging our linked hands. As our voices mingled together in the gathering darkness, I was free from life's nitty-gritty details, from my body, from heavy thoughts. As if little by little my flesh and bones lost weight, as if my body had turned into a hollow sky lantern that could rise with the slightest heat. I could fly wherever I wanted if I cut the string loose. Nobody could tie me down. I was convinced in those moments that I was born to sing, that I couldn't live without singing.

I can't forget the evening in April when I took part in an outdoor performance for the first time. We had just finished performing our repertoire when, out of the blue, Meejin Sunbae began singing solo. Passersby stopped in their tracks, and my fellow band members and I turned toward her. Her clear, soft voice had determination, and had a story of its own independent of melody and lyrics. When her song entered me, sharp yet gentle, a piece of me I had struggled to hide and keep secret and wished to ignore surfaced against my will. I didn't know what it was exactly, but her song made me feel both ashamed and sad. I wanted to push my hands against her frail shoulders and press my lips on hers. I wanted to flow into that small mouth, into that darkness. I was desperate to be nearer to her world, even by just a step. This was before we became close.

We walked through the Summer Garden together. Warm sunlight shone on the crowns of our heads.

"Didn't you find it hard to live in Russia?" I asked.

"At first I just wanted to go back to Korea. There, I thought I was on the smart side at school, but here I was one of the worst students. That took me by surprise. I couldn't speak the language, so. I would've given up midway if I hadn't met Julia. She helped me a lot. We were similar in many ways. Both of us were hot-tempered." Blue veins were conspicuous against Sunbae's pale arm.

"You should see the sun from time to time. You look like a walking white rice cake," I said disapprovingly, at which Sunbae let out a long yawn and mumbled, "I want to eat rice cake."

"Why are you still using formal Korean with me anyway? You call Soohyun and the other girls 'Unni' and you use informal Korean with them," Sunbae said when we reached the riverside.

"I don't know. Back then I just felt we were ages apart in our enrollment year, and you were someone I looked up to. You seemed so grown-up that I didn't dare drop my formal Korean with you. And you weren't exactly approachable, either."

The other Sunbaes had treated me as the precious frosh, but

not Meejin Sunbae. She never talked to me first, and when I entered the band room she packed her bag and swept out without saying bye or see you later or anything. When I bumped into her on the street and said hello, she would give me a curt nod with a wooden expression and walk off as if she wanted to avoid me. It was only when I got to know her later that I understood her behavior as the best an introvert with no conversation skills could muster.

"Sunbae, why were you like that back then?" I asked, and she gave me an embarrassed grin. I had loved, hated, and misunderstood that face for a long time. We sat awhile on a bench without speaking, watching the sunlight undulate across the Neva River.

"Did you have a good time with Meejin?" Julia asked.

"Yes. I went near her research office and dropped by the Summer Garden, then walked all the way to the river and back."

A petite Asian woman came over holding the menu and spoke to Julia in Russian.

"She's asking who you are, if you're Meejin's little sister. So I said you're her friend. And that you arrived yesterday from Seoul." The woman looked at me and said this and that in Russian. "She thought you were family because you look like Meejin. She hopes you have a good trip in St. Petersburg and says not to take the subway at night. Says it's dangerous." I said thank you in

Russian. We ate stir-fry noodles and spring rolls before slowly heading back to Julia's apartment.

"**I don't remember** why I fought with Meejin anymore," said Julia. "At one point I hated her so much that, after saying a bunch of hurtful things to her, I was sure I wouldn't shed a tear if she died in front of me. I screamed at her to get out of my house while she was still packing her stuff in her big suitcase." Julia paused, too distraught to say more.

"That can happen. That can happen with anyone, Julia. She told me it was thanks to you that she was able to settle in Russia. She told me that many times. She was so grateful." Julia smiled faintly at my words.

"There was a lot of misunderstanding between us because we spoke in Russian, which was a foreign language for both of us. Our cultures were different, too, so what Meejin said as a joke sometimes felt like an insult to me. She probably felt the same way. We went everywhere together since we both had no one else to rely on. Naturally, we began to expect things from each other and our disappointment grew that much greater. No matter how hard I try, I can't really remember why we fought so much near the end. I guess little fights added up, but I don't know why I lashed out at her like that for something I can't even remember."

"For her part, she probably feels sorry about a lot of things, too. I also know her, Julia. She's hotheaded. And doesn't know how to fake her emotions."

"So true, so true." Julia nodded, beaming. "She must've had her work cut out for her. I mean, Korean and Russian are two completely different languages. Her experience would've been worlds apart from a Pole learning Russian. It would've been even harder for her because she started late, and she was proud, too. Her pride really got on my nerves back then, but, looking back, I think that's why I liked her."

It was my turn to nod. We sat at Julia's kitchen table, sharing several glasses of orange juice spiked with vodka. The conversation often halted, and when we resumed we were looking at different places.

"You are nothing," said Julia. "Has anyone ever told you that, Soeun? I've been told that many times since I was a child. You are nothing. My own father was the one who said it." As she spoke, she gazed quietly at the dried flowers hanging on the wall. "Soeun. The thing about children is, they believe and accept everything an adult says. They live with those words for the rest of their lives. You are nothing. You are nothing, my father would tell me. You're a useless brat. A big, useless brat. I didn't want to be seen, but my body kept developing. I walked around with a slouch hoping that hunching my shoulders would make me look a bit smaller, but it was no use. I wanted to disappear. That's why when a Russian man proposed to me, I married him and came here like a runaway. I couldn't leave him even when he treated me with contempt or swore at me for no reason. I must've thought he'd done me the huge favor of marrying me when I was nothing." A bitter smile crossed Julia's face.

"Meejin came to see the apartment when I was in a mess after splitting with him. We decided to live together, and we sat talking at this table every night. She'd only been in Russia for a year then and was having a difficult time. I gladly offered her help whenever she asked. I accompanied her to the immigration office and her school; I acted as her spokesperson for things she couldn't explain in Russian. She was grateful to me. Looking back, I think at the time I liked to see myself helping someone weaker than I was. I said we were friends yet considered myself to be above her. I thought: you can't do anything without me. I grew angrier at her the better her Russian got, the less she needed my help, the more she hung out with other, more charming friends. I felt like she was telling me, You are nothing. You are nothing. I couldn't stand it. I realized only after she left that what I'd thought to be selflessness was actually selfishness."

I spotted Sunbae in front of Dostoevsky's house. She was leaning against a wall in navy blue shorts and a white crewneck, carrying a black backpack. The wind blew, revealing the face veiled beneath her hair each time. The expression on her face was like a child's.

We didn't say a word to each other as we walked quietly

around Dostoevsky's house. The table clock was set to the time of his death, and the portraits he had drawn of his children hung on the walls. A roulette set, a game he had been addicted to his entire life, was also on display. Sunbae pointed at Dostoevsky's belongings without a word, casting intermittent glances my way. We stood before his portrait for a long time. It was the same portrait placed on Sunbae's desk when we used to live together. Dostoevsky had brought us together under the name "friends" despite the wide gap in our enrollment year, despite our strong personalities and sensitive temperaments that made it hard for us to make friends.

When Sunbae told me she was going to Russia to study Dostoevsky's novels, I knew instinctively that she would never return to Korea. She said she would finish in seven years at most, but I couldn't take her words at face value. I kept telling myself that I could see her again at any time, but deep down I thought it was over between us.

We lived together for three years right up to Sunbae's departure for Russia. The day before she moved out, I took out a big chunk of my savings from my part-time job to buy groceries and make her favorite dishes. I served meatless dumplings, gimbap, bean sprout soup, japchae, tofu salad, caramelized sweet potatoes, and watermelon punch. I remember watching her chew an enormous piece of gimbap she had stuffed in her mouth and worrying whether she would be able to eat properly in a foreign land. Sitting in her empty room after she left, forcing down leftover japchae, I didn't cry. I felt no sadness. Only helpless worry over what she could eat in Russia when she couldn't eat meat. Using such seemingly reasonable worries to cover up and deceive my deep loss and sadness was nothing new to me.

I had never talked to Sunbae directly even until the school festival in May. She always sat at a different table from me whenever we ate out with the band, and Homecoming Day was no exception.

She sat diagonally across from me at the next table, in the basement of the bar we went to for the homecoming after-party. I had wanted to sit beside her, but as people sat in the order they arrived, I wound up squeezed between the Sunbaes who attended our school in the eighties and nineties. In front of me sat two Sunbaes who looked positively exhausted. Their tired faces belied their disgruntlement with the gathering.

"So you enrolled in '02?" the curly-haired one asked. When I nodded, he took out a business card from his pocket. It read, "Patent Attorney Shin Gyungsok." "I enrolled back in '86," he said, scrutinizing me as he did so. Uncomfortable, I averted my gaze, but when I glanced back his eyes were still fixed on me. It didn't take long for my discomfort to turn into irritation.

"Why does the frosh look so glum? You're a Korean lit major, I hear. So am I—I enrolled in '95. The name's Kim Yeonsook," said the female Sunbae sitting next to the patent attorney

Sunbae, handing me her business card. She was a journalist for Newspaper K.

That day, the mood during drinks was strange from the outset. The alumni Sunbaes drank fast and traded barbed jokes with one another. What they said felt closer to attacks than jokes—I perceived this from their tone and the mood, but the details of their conversation were lost on me. Terms like *stance* or *National Liberation* or *People's Democracy* or *betrayal*. They began to taunt each other using the foulest insults, and the mood grew so contentious that the Sunbaes from the enrollment year '99 had to break up the fight. The Sunbaes at my table paid no heed, as if this were a perfectly normal situation.

"Our band tends to attract people full of piss and vinegar. There's too much talk and trouble and they squabble as soon as they're drunk," said the journalist Sunbae, almost yelling. "Isn't it too loud in here, Sunbae? Can't tell if we're talking or shouting."

Eminem's rap was blaring from the speaker.

"Who picked this place for the after-party? I expected better from band kids," said the patent attorney Sunbae. His gaze lingered on my hands and probed my apricot-painted nails. He had a look of disapproval. "College students were intellectuals back in the day. Kids these days, though, they dye their hair and paint their nails and they're so intoxicated by pop culture that they've no idea how great their Sunbaes' achievements are." He leaned against the wall, puffing on a cigarette. While he talked to the journalist Sunbae, I looked over at Meejin Sunbae. For the first time, she met my gaze and sent me a supportive look. At least that's how I remember it.

"Hey, Youngjae. Go tell the owner to turn down the music. It's giving me a headache," the journalist Sunbae bellowed to a Sunbae from the enrollment year of '99 who was sitting next to me. When the music quieted down, the patent attorney Sunbae, who had been chugging soju in rapid succession, began complaining, "When did I ever ask to be respected for my seniority? I just wanted our band to continue in a healthy way. But look at this wreck. The way I see it, your club has no future, none at all."

The Sunbae from the enrollment year of '99 was busily pouring soju into his Sunbaes' empty glasses, nodding at the patent attorney Sunbae's words. The journalist Sunbae chimed in, "That's so true, Hyung. Have you seen the girls at our school? They go everywhere in groups like silly schoolgirls, calling their Sunbae 'Oppa.' If you ask me, our band's in this mess now because we didn't have guys join to provide strong leadership. I'm a woman, too, but I know that girls can't band together or understand how an organization works." She paused and shot me a look. "Your name is Soeun, yeah?" When I nodded, she went on, "This goes to you as well. If you count yourself as part of our band, don't you think you should lose the feminine attitude? The way you talk, the way you dress . . . I'm a woman, but I've seen so many women out in the real world who just can't fit in. They get pouty for everything, they whine and fuss. Men don't do that. Why do you think us college women are special? We're the third gender. We are women, but we should reject what's inferior about other women. I'm telling you this because I'm your Sunbae, who else would? If no one tells you, you're going to get slammed out there in the real world, you know."

My dyed, bright brown hair, my manicured nails and reedy voice, my shy, introverted personality, even my gender as a woman . . . I sat there, seized by the feeling that everything about me was being denied.

"What, you're offended? What's with the look on your face?" the journalist Sunbae asked. Without answering, I glanced at Meejin Sunbae. She gave me a faint smile. Her mouth was smiling, but in her eyes I read cold rage.

"Guys *are* easier to deal with. In my day, if we didn't like a junior we used to stand them in a corner and beat them up with a baseball bat. That was all education, you know," the patent attorney Sunbae remarked.

"Bullshit." It was Meejin Sunbae.

"What did you say?" the patent attorney Sunbae asked in a low voice.

"I said, bullshit," Meejin Sunbae answered in the polite form. The Sunbaes two tables over who had been bickering even until then looked our way and fell silent. Heh, the patent attorney Sunbae let out a disbelieving laugh. "You dare? When 'Your Sunbae is your sky'?"

"Are we not allowed to talk now?" said Meejin Sunbae, a curious smile playing across her face.

"Meejin, Gyungsok Hyung is just fond of the newbie and is giving her good advice. Hyung, you know how Meejin is, she's a bit touchy. Meejin, apologize to Gyungsok Hyung, and the other Hyungs." The journalist Sunbae grasped Meejin Sunbae's arm.

"Let go of me." Meejin Sunbae yanked her arm free. "Is enrollment year some kind of medal? Is the prick who shows up every year, gets drunk, and picks on the youngest, weakest girl still my Sunbae? Shin Gyungsok, you say you love democracy? How can someone who has to tower over weaker people, even in this little group, go on about democracy? I bet a guy like you would feel right at home in a dictatorship. Even the *idea* of everyone being equal is beyond you, honestly. Fuck, do we really have to make *her* watch this shitshow, too? I don't want to do that anymore, I refuse."

"You've always been so emotional. That's your weakness, and if you can't overcome that, you won't survive in the workplace," said the journalist Sunbae.

"Mind your own business, Kim Yeonsook," said Meejin Sunbae. "Is being a woman really that embarrassing and painful? Women are emotional, disruptive, selfish, and therefore more likely to betray the organization; a woman's enemy is another woman. Is that sort of self-denial the healthiness you talk of? You should be ashamed in front of your female juniors." Sunbae's voice was shaking violently. She grabbed her bag with trembling hands and stormed out. Frantically, I put on my backpack and hurried after her.

When I went out into the street, Sunbae was already standing before the crosswalk at the roundabout.

"Meejin Sunbae."

She didn't look around.

"Sunbae."

I drew nearer and peered up at her face. She was smiling oddly, but when I looked closer, she was crying. I took out a tissue from my backpack and handed it to her. She wiped her tears with it, crossed the street, and walked away. I wouldn't have spoken to her if I knew she was crying. I felt bad, thinking I had upset her without meaning to.

It was only much later that I learned she was being blamed for ending the tradition of student activism in our band. She was in the band at a time when student activism, which had already been losing momentum, was rapidly collapsing. She challenged one by one the strict hierarchy between senior and junior students, the predominance of male students in the leadership body, and the culture of obedience, whereupon the older band members grew sick of her. She was accused of being hung up on what in their eyes were hardly problems and was even criticizing their methods of activism when it was hard enough to carry on the legacy of "the Hyungs," or "the brotherhood," as a united group. Few people, I heard, looked kindly upon her for that. Some even wished she would leave the band and abandon her campaign for the autonomous decision-making of individuals, equal relationships, and feminist pedagogy. They alluded to sayings like "If a monk doesn't like the temple, the monk can simply leave"—and yet she clung on, refusing to quit the band.

Now that I think of it, for all the comments she got about being intractable and hard as nails, Sunbae was only in her early twenties at the time. She must've been hurt, even if she had resolved to endure the hate of many people. How much courage had she needed to fight from within an organization that did not support and respect her? The tears shed by the twenty-five-year-old Sunbae at the roundabout crosswalk that day might not have been rage, but the accumulation of her loneliness.

"I think it was three months after you left for Russia," I said, "that the band broke up."

"That sounds about right," Sunbae replied.

"There were Sunbaes who flat-out blamed us. Though most people didn't even show their disappointment. I felt like I'd single-handedly destroyed a space that contained their memories."

"It couldn't be helped. It really couldn't. Not when the world had changed." Sunbae was looking at her shadow, hands tucked in her pants pockets. Slowly, we strolled down the alley behind Dostoevsky's house.

"Twenty-, twenty-one-year-olds started university and finally got to debate what had happened in Gwangju in May, how ill our society was. They sang because they were hurt and distressed. Some Sunbaes said singing was a tool to educate, a means to galvanize, but I think our songs were a promise we made to ourselves. The promise that I, at least, won't live a life of pursuing darkness. The joy of being able to sing together—I think that was enough. I didn't want our songs to sound like the national anthem sung before the Korean flag at school assemblies." Sunbae's voice was shaking slightly. Her voice always shook a little whenever she spoke from the heart. She told me once that she wanted to fix her weak habit of letting her speech betray her feelings. She was ashamed of the trembling in her voice when she became emotionally vulnerable, of her unsociable personality, of her tendency to walk slowly and eat slowly and read slowly, of her poor athletic skills, of her sensitivity that made her extract a hundred meanings from someone's words or actions and chew over them endlessly. She had to overcome such weaknesses, she said, and become a new person. I didn't know what she thought her own strengths were, but I loved the things she considered her weaknesses; they also made me smile a lot.

We had almost reached the Orthodox cathedral we meant to visit when a sudden shower of rain fell, forcing us to take refuge in a café opposite the cathedral. The city was sweat-inducingly hot on sunny days, but, being wet from the rain, we felt a chill as soon as we stepped into the cool indoors.

"Is your writing going well?" she asked.

"Not so well. I'm scared."

"What's there to be scared about?"

"Make one mistake and I might lose my chance forever. What I dread most is writing a work so bad that I can't even defend it." I remembered publishing a failed story recently and being too ashamed and scared to even cry. Harsh reviews sprang up online, with definitive pronouncements that clung to me as I wrote, that seemed to tell me my writing would never improve in the slightest. I recalled a friend's advice to deliver at least a "base hit" with every publication. If I produced a foul ball even after my dutiful hours at the desk, I would have no way to defend myself. The thought that I couldn't predict where my ball would go until I batted was paralyzing.

"I remember the story you showed me. Before I left for Russia."

"You read it and told me to give up writing. That I shouldn't go out of my way to take the hard road, that I should make my life easier. And this came from someone who was going to Russia to study nineteenth-century fiction." I laughed.

"Do I come up in your writing?"

"Whatever I write, I think of you, Sunbae. Look carefully. It's all you."

"How's your health?"

"I can manage without medication now. I get a lot of sun, I sleep a ton. Really, I'm fine now."

Back when I was very sick, Sunbae emailed me almost every day. When I wrote that the medication wasn't working too well, she instantly replied that she knew someone who had taken the same medication and recovered, that Prozac was an effective drug, even if it could take a while to work. She called internationally if I didn't respond to her email. Soeun, she would say, calling my name. Sometimes I broke down and sobbed upon hearing that one word; other times, when she told me I would get better, I would shake violently, blustering that she should hang up if she was going to give me superficial reassurances.

I remember my illness as a foul odor on my breath. An odor that wouldn't leave my body no matter how many times I brushed my teeth or showered. It was hard to drag myself out of bed every morning and, at times, walking to the bathroom felt impossible. My attitude toward life, which was characterized by a diligence bordering on self-torture, did not help at all when it came to that illness. Showering, blow-drying, getting dressed, and heading out the door consumed a full day's worth of physical strength and willpower. I was not the master of my own body.

From a window in the hospital corridor, I could see Marronnier Park across the street. Was the twenty-, twenty-one-year-old me who sang my heart out perched on that park's wall truly the same person as the twenty-four-year-old me who kept slumping to the ground even when I stood still, because my knees gave from the side effects of medication? My memories of singing at Marronnier Park, the sound of that song, the laughter, I lost it all. Like a train that cuts off its tail end by accident and hurtles for-

ward, I lost the person I had known to be me. Twenty-year-old me
split off cleanly from twenty-four-year-old me and was left standing alone on a dark railway, to which I could never return.

Sunbae was having a rough time of her own settling down in
Russia, but to me her difficulties were simply and literally someone else's business. I was the most hurt, the most agonized person in the world, so my eyes saw nothing but my own pain. That
selfishness, I think, contained neither love for Sunbae nor love
for myself. The me back then had no energy to love. But Sunbae
had never stopped loving me, and I didn't know what to say to
her now after so long.

Mass was taking place inside the cathedral. As it was an Orthodox church that wasn't furnished with pews, the entire congregation observed the Mass standing except for the few people who
had mobility difficulties and sat on wall-mounted seats. When
the cantor started off a song, the congregation joined in. Though
a small cathedral, the ceiling dome produced deep echoes of the
singing. Sunbae stood at the very back and sang Mass with the
rest of the congregation. Gospodi pomiluj, Gospodi pomiluj,
Gospodi pomiluj. I wondered how Sunbae could sing Mass
when she wasn't even Orthodox Christian, but her voice, mingled with other voices, drummed at my heart. Lord have mercy,
Lord have mercy. She sang standing close to me. I heard the clap

of thunder, the drum of heavy raindrops against the cathedral roof. Gospodi pomiluj, Gospodi pomiluj, Gospodi pomiluj. I began to sing along, stumbling over the words. Her voice and mine blended seamlessly into the resonances.

When the rain stopped, we left the cathedral and walked to the Fontanka River. A pleasure boat sailed by carrying a group of tourists, who waved at us and we at them. Why did people on boats wave to people on land? We sat on a low wall near the river and watched the golden dome of St. Isaac's Cathedral opposite us. Streetlamps lit up and the passing boat switched on its lights, too.

"I hope you never have to suffer like that again," Sunbae said. "I hope you don't live life too seriously. Even if it isn't easy to do, I hope you'll at least remember that you are someone who can sing. I can't do anything for you, Soeun, but . . ." She began to sing her old favorite song. In the voice that had once made me feel both sad and ashamed. She looked at me as she sang, her face glowing radiant as it once had.

Sunbae never lived to my current age.

The song ended, and I heard the sound of people clapping. I turned off the cassette player and took the earphones out of my ears. I heard the sound of cars driving by, the sound of fireworks in the distance. The streetlamps spilled light onto the river.

In the summer of 2009, Sunbae's heart stopped without reason. She was supposed to have her dissertation defense soon and had no special health issues other than chronic fatigue. She had died at the age of thirty-two, far away from home. The doctor said she would not have felt any pain, as she had suffered an instant heart attack. That she had died painlessly offered only small comfort to the many people who were wounded by her death. She had had many enemies. All the people who had loathed her and bristled at the mere mention of her name came to the funeral, one by one, and hung their heads.

In my hand were a few pictures of Sunbae that Julia had given me. Sunbae eating ice cream at the Summer Garden, Sunbae smiling with her eyes closed on a bench by the Neva River, Sunbae leaning on a wall of Dostoevsky's house waiting for Julia, Sunbae sitting on the terrace of a café trying to say something, Sunbae standing on a path by the Fontanka, smiling and waving to tourists aboard a boat. I chased Sunbae this way and that, seeing through Julia's gaze.

Goodbye, Sunbae. I remembered Sunbae's face when she stood before that crosswalk once upon a time, desperately holding back tears; it dawned on me that my face was now the same way, ever since I lost her. And that I had been wishing to become the driest, the most detached person I could be.

Goodbye, Soeun. The day I met Sunbae for the last time, I couldn't smile at her when she bid me farewell. Her advice that I shouldn't live life too seriously had sounded like an infantilizing lecture to me. She had gone out of her way to come to Korea when I was finally starting to break free of my disease, yet I didn't even thank her. It was because I felt inferior to her, who was always so grown-up compared to the immature, sick, inadequate mess that

I was. I treated her that way despite knowing, in my head, that I couldn't have made it through that time without her affection.

For her endless interest in and advice for me, I was grateful as I was increasingly resentful. I felt that she was trampling on the boundaries of "me," rudely trespassing on the space that was "me." She was far away yet much too close to me. I couldn't stand her love, which did not reject even the ugliest of my faces. I couldn't stand it because I had been afraid of being loved from the beginning.

"This might sound strange," Julia began, "but when I first met Meejin, she said she regretted moving here for her studies. She explained that a friend she'd lived with fell ill shortly after she left. I told her it wasn't her fault, but she blamed herself. She saved bus fares, avoided eating out as much as possible—I wondered what she was saving up for, and it turned out she was trying to go back to Korea during her school break. She just wanted to meet her friend and cook for her, listen to her, stay by her side. That was all she could think about. When she came back from Korea, she said her friend was doing much better, and she felt less troubled to be back after seeing her friend improve. I'm guessing that friend is you, Soeun?"

I nodded. It was true I had been getting better, but I was still unquestionably a patient at the time and couldn't face Sunbae with a smile. She had asked me to visit St. Petersburg the following summer and I had said nothing.

"What did Meejin say about me?" Julia asked.

"She said you were special, Julia. Not because you helped her or were competent, you just were. She'd never seen someone like you. And . . ."

"She said that?"

And you don't know it, she said, which pained her. You told me the other night that you live with the thought that you're nothing. When you said it, I felt like she was sitting right next to me. Like she was saying, 'That's not true, Julia,' with a sigh."

Julia lowered her head, eyes red, and fiddled with the tablecloth. "I thought I'd see her again soon. Meejin only lived twenty minutes away by bus. I thought I'd just give her a call and we'd grab dinner together. But I was scared she might still be mad at me. If I'd plucked up a bit more courage, I could've contacted her before she died. Our friendship may not have gone back to what it once was, but at least I wouldn't have so much regret. Would she have waited for me to get in touch? Wouldn't she have been sad the whole time because we parted that way? It's painful to have these thoughts."

"She wouldn't want you to be tied to the past and suffer."

"Right, Meejin wouldn't want that."

Julia stared at the photographs of Sunbae that were lying on the table.

"Meejin, I miss you," Julia said quietly, hugging the photographs to her chest. "I keep forgetting you bit by bit. Now I can't really remember what you looked like, Meejin." I put my arms around Julia as she called Sunbae's name. Julia's body was big and warm. In our embrace, I felt Sunbae giving Julia a hug. I heard her voice comfort Julia from inside my body: Julia, Julia, I'm sorry I left like that.

I took out a cassette tape from my bag. Scribbled on it were the words "Kim Meejin, enrollment year '97." I inserted the tape into a boom box and pressed play. I heard the distant honking of cars. Then the sound of Sunbae clearing her throat, of her singing do-re-mi-fa-sol to choose a key. Julia came over to sit closer to the boom box.

"Testing, testing, this is Russian lit major Kim Meejin, enrolled in '97. Our Sunbaes recently bought a recorder for the band. They told me I can hear my own voice better by listening to a recording of it. With more practice, I hope to be a good singer, too." Sunbae's speech was greeted by peals of laughter from the band. That's the spirit, frosh, sing us a song then, sing us your favorite song.

My young, twenty-year-old Sunbae sang "Mung Bean Flower" [녹두꽃] in the crystal-clear voice of an innocent. She was singing in a corner of a small apartment in St. Petersburg, in a voice that still tugged at my heart. Julia and I sat side by side in front of the boom box and listened to the story Sunbae was telling. The song ended, followed by the sound of applause and Sunbae's laughter.

Sunbae sang songs by Nochatsa [노찾사], Kkotdaji [꽃다지],

and Jang Sa-ik [장사익], as well as some Bob Marley and Billie Holiday. The tape also included her singing Michael Jackson and Latin hymns. Whatever she sang, whosever song she sang, she made it her own. Her voice, which had a husky timbre when she spoke, acquired a clarity and tenderness as soon as she began to sing. There was no technique in her singing. She didn't belt out certain parts for emphasis or employ the ubiquitous vibrato. She didn't plead. She sang a sad song dryly, a fiery song calmly.

I hadn't dared listen to the songs up until then for fear of losing my self-control. I had also dreaded stepping on St. Petersburgian soil, where Sunbae had died. I had wanted my emotions to stay like carefully stacked plates instead of crashing down, paranoid that their shards might stab and upset my insides. That was when Julia took my hand. She found out my email address and began to write to me. Now I wrote about the Sunbae I had lived with, now Julia wrote about the Sunbae she had lived with. We were both talking about Sunbae, but inevitably I talked about myself and she, herself. For the past year, I had written to a Polish woman I had never met as though I were writing in my diary.

I heard the sound of a motorbike scrape the road as it passed, the occasional whirring of the refrigerator. Julia and I had been avoiding eye contact but at some point started looking at each other in the face. The last track was "Mung Bean Flower" sung by me and Sunbae together. Twenty-three-year-old me and twenty-eight-year-old Sunbae sang, putting the hottest, most beautiful heart we had in us into that poetry. Back when I hadn't been a patient and she the deceased, back when we hadn't been anything yet. In this manner we parted.

A gentle headwind blew onto the living room floor where Julia and I sat facing each other. Like Julia, I was slowly forgetting Sunbae. The feelings I'd had while singing this song with her were faint now. I was out of my mind for half a year after she left, but my grief, my yearning for her that was closer to rage, had paled over time. After the song ended, I listened to the tape rolling for a while then pushed the stop button. Julia, whose face was flushed, was trying her best to smile at me. The song had ended, and we were left with time that Sunbae didn't have.

We decided to go on a boat cruise the next day. We agreed to lean over the rails of the boat and wave as hard as we could at the people passing by on bridges and roads. It would be Julia's and my first journey together.

Michaela

1

She looked down at the people from the window. Catholic worshippers sat on roads normally occupied by buses and cars, attending Mass. In the distance, the Pope was presiding over the Mass at Gwanghwamun Square as the crowd in attendance thronged the entire Gwanghwamun and Jongno areas.

"We're going to meet at five a.m. and leave. I heard it'll take quite a while to find a spot even after we arrive in Seoul."

Her mom had been as excited as a child going on a picnic, urging her to look for her outside the window since the Mass might take place near her office. She pressed her forehead against the window and scanned the crowd, but all she could see from the fifteenth floor was waves of white veils.

"You won't even get a clear view of the Pope's face—I bet you'll see him better on TV. You really want to go through all that trouble from the break of dawn?"

"You don't know what you're talking about. I'm attending a Mass presided over by the Holy Father, and with so many other congregants, too. I'll never have another chance like this in my life. How thankful I am, Michaela dear."

Twenty-five years ago, she followed her mom to Seoul to attend a Mass presided over by a Poland-born Pope. It took place in the old Yeouido Square, apparently drawing 650,000 worshippers. What she remembered about that day was the taste of the plum candy her mom had popped into her mouth. Her mom had bitten down on the candy and pushed it into her mouth, piece by piece, lest she choke on it. The day had been warm with hints of autumn chill, and she had fallen asleep drooling sweet saliva on her mom's bosom. Her mom's satin hanbok had felt crisp against her cheek.

Her mom hung a photograph from that day on the living room wall. The photograph showed her mom smiling in a cherry-pink hanbok and white veil, next to whom she was standing with a scowl. Wearing white tights and a white dress, which her mom had managed to borrow after calling up every single friend in the neighborhood, she was clutching the hem of her mom's dress, still half asleep.

Her mom looked at the photograph and talked about how lovely the weather had been that day, how beautiful the procession of priests in their white vestments, how enormous the blessing her family had received. There were many people who couldn't attend despite wanting to, her mom reminded her, so she should know how much God loved her, how much God gave her, and be thankful even in moments of sadness.

Her mom was always like that. Thankful that the kimchi ripened well, thankful that the price of pork dropped enough for her to eat her fill, thankful that the wart on her toe healed, thankful that God granted her the health to work, thankful that she could eat out, thankful that when things didn't go well, they taught her to be thankful when things did go well.

But in that litany of thanks, Michaela perceived only her mom's bleak reality: her mom wouldn't need to be especially thankful for eating out if she were able to do so anytime. She wouldn't need to be thankful for a drop in pork prices if she were always able to eat as much pork as she liked. If she had money, if she had wealthy parents or a rich husband, she wouldn't need to be thankful for being able to stand and work ten hours every day through physical pain. Michaela would rather her mom be honest about her situation and complain; her mom's gratitude for the wretchedness of reality had, for a while, felt deceitful.

By the time she finished work and looked out the window, everyone had gone and the only occupants of the road were cars. She was watching people stroll down sidewalks when she suddenly wondered where her mom was.

"I'll stay at a girlfriend's place. She used to live in our neighborhood before she moved to Seoul. You wouldn't know her. How thankful I am for her."

Her mom intended to close the hair salon for three days and go sightseeing in Seoul. The plan was to attend the Pope's Mass on Saturday, then on Sunday and Monday visit Myeongdong, Namsan Tower, and the 63 Building, and if possible take a boat cruise along the Han River. She resented her mom for tactlessly turning up in Seoul without considering how busy she was.

She pinned her hopes on the "girlfriend" her mom had mentioned. Maybe her mom would sightsee with that friend. She hadn't been asked to come along after all. Seeing as her mom hadn't called her after the Mass, the two women had probably met up already and gone to the friend's house.

Her mom had come to her place in Seoul just once. As she had lived with a roommate until she was twenty-seven, it was only when she got her own place that her mom was able to visit. On that occasion, her mom brought an icebox laden with marinated meat, spicy braised pollack, pickled perilla leaves, chili powder, radish kimchi, and sesame oil. Her mom would have carried that heavy load while transferring from bus to train to subway in order to see her, but, far from feeling grateful, her chest felt heavy with frustration.

"How is this fridge so tiny?" her mom sighed in front of the mini fridge, which was loaded with beer cans. "What will we do with all this food? Even chili powder attracts bugs if you don't keep it in the fridge." Her mom opened the airtight container into which she had packed the meat, sniffed it, and said, "We'll have to finish this today, Michaela dear."

The two of them had grilled meat all through lunch and dinner.

Even though she was full, her mom forced her to eat more, insisting they eat up the meat before it went bad. Her mom emptied the mini fridge of every beer can and filled it with the spicy braised pollack, pickled perilla leaves, chili powder, and radish kimchi, all of which had been transferred into plastic bags. When the door of the overflowing fridge wouldn't close, her mom told her to take out a few chunks of pollack and eat them. So she ate that, too.

Not even staying the night, her mom made to set off again to catch the train. The woman didn't know how to rest. The monthly rent for her salon was rising yet she charged the same price for haircuts and perms as ten years ago, so she obviously wasn't turning a profit. Even when Michaela offered to take her to Seoul Station at least, she was adamant about going alone, telling her to use that time to catch up on some sleep. Michaela suffered acute indigestion after her mom left. She vomited everything she had eaten but, still getting chills and drenched in sweat, finally had to go to the emergency room.

Her mom really didn't know how to be considerate.

2

Michaela didn't call. Was she too busy? It was only when the woman mopped her sweaty forehead with the sleeves of her hanbok that she remembered it had been borrowed. She began to think, as she waited for the Mass, that she might need to pay for the jeogori jacket. Armpit sweat ran down the jeogori, which she had to return clean, and by noon left a hideous stain.

This hanbok, which she had borrowed from her Legion of Mary sister, was no ordinary hanbok. It had been given to the sister for her son's wedding, from the parents of her daughter-in-law. A high-quality gown consisting of an indigo dress and a chick-yellow jeogori jacket. The sister had apparently never even taken it out of the closet except to wear to Mass on solemnities, but had gladly lent it to her for the papal Mass. The woman told herself she would need to reimburse the sister if dry cleaning didn't erase the stain. A duffel bag was slung on her shoulder. Now she had to look for a place to sleep.

She had told people at church that she would sleep at Michaela's place in Seoul and tour the city properly for the first time in her life, including a visit to Namsan Tower and even a boat cruise. People said Michaela, though cold on the outside, was kind at heart. That her daughter made up for her lifetime of hardship.

They were right. Michaela had always been a daughter she could count on. She felt both gratitude and pity for her daughter, who had put down her roots in Seoul all on her own after much struggle. The woman couldn't afford to send Michaela to a single cram school when every other parent did, and had bought her school uniform from the street market instead of name-brand tailors. Her savings had paid Michaela's college admission fee and first-semester tuition, but nothing beyond that. Michaela had come home during the first summer break and announced she would work her way through school, telling the woman to stop working herself to the bone.

The woman felt shame whenever she thought of such a daughter. Her guilt at having done nothing for her kid made her resolve not to be a burden at least. She was putting 300,000 won each month toward a savings account to pay for Michaela's future marriage and planned to continue saving after that to prepare for her own retirement.

"I'm not getting married, Mom," Michaela had declared from a young age.

"Girls who say that are the first ones to marry, you know."

It had been adorable whenever her daughter said those words with that sulky face of hers. But when Michaela said the same thing even after she turned thirty, the woman began to feel a little frightened that her daughter might be serious.

No one would have made a better bride than her Michaela. The girl had graduated from a university in Seoul, gotten a job there, and was resourceful enough to have earned the hefty deposit for her rented room. While her personality wasn't especially amiable, she was polite and articulate and spoke with the refinement of someone who had studied in Seoul. If she wished, Michaela would've already gotten herself a rich man *and* borne two babies by now.

The woman couldn't understand why Michaela chose instead to take the path of thorns. Lurking at the end of that thought was a twinge of guilt: was she the one holding back her daughter? After all, she wasn't good enough to be Michaela's mother.

She set out for the subway. Her plan was to find accommodation in Mangwon-dong, where her daughter lived. Perhaps Michaela would call tomorrow morning and they'd have lunch together; she lacked the courage to call Michaela first. The child was working on Independence Day and now a Saturday, wasn't she? The woman didn't wish to pressure the busy girl. Her hope had been to see her daughter's face at least once, but even that seemed too selfish of her. With great effort, she quieted her heart.

There had been a time when she could see her daughter to her heart's desire. She came home from work to a daughter who shouted "Mom!" in delight and rushed toward her. Hugging her daughter eased all the pain away, giving her the strength to work once more the following day. Who else in the world would love her so? Fly into her arms with such a bright, pretty face?

Those days had gone, but she could not forget the love she had received from Michaela. People said that your debt to your parents was as immense as the sky, but she felt, on the contrary, that the love your children gave you was like the sky. The affection young Michaela had given her was a warm, devoted love she would find nowhere else in the world.

The motel, which resembled a run-down Chinese restaurant, cost 80,000 won a night. The man at the reception desk eyed her suspiciously as he repeated, "I said it's 80,000 won. Weekend rates."

She scanned the pricing table stuck to the glass partition in front of the desk. As the man had said, weeknights cost 60,000 won, weekends 80,000 won. Not for nothing did people say Seoul prices were murder. She tried two more motels close by, which charged just as much as the first one or even more. Her feet were swelling inside her kkotsin shoes. She tightly retied the half bow of her jeogori that had come undone, and walked to a nearby bus stop. The sweat soaking her armpits had now reached her cuffs. The jeogori would have to be paid for now. She couldn't even begin to guess how much it had cost.

On the bus stop bench, she asked a middle-aged woman sitting next to her, "Are there any jjimjilbangs around here?"

"Take the bus that I'm taking. I'll tell you where it is since I'll get off after you. Are you here for a wedding? Where are you coming from?"

She had been wary because she expected all Seoulites to be snooty, but relaxed upon meeting someone who answered her and offered help. She proudly told the middle-aged woman that she had gone to a Mass presided over by the Holy Father today. In fact, she added, it was her second time getting an audience with the Holy Father. Her chest swelled. "I attended the Mass at Yeouido Square in '89. Back then, His Holiness Pope John Paul II—"

"But why aren't you going back with the other church folks?" the middle-aged woman cut her off. She didn't seem very interested in the Holy Father.

"I have to meet someone."

"Ah, you must not have any children in Seoul. Even so, you're going to a jjimjilbang dressed up like that?"

"Oh, no, that's not—"

"This is it, this is your stop." The middle-aged woman almost pushed her out of the bus. Waving at the departing bus, she thought that not all Seoulites were snooty, after all.

3

Her mom didn't call.

How happy she must've been yesterday. How many times she must've shouted thankful-thankful for being able to celebrate Mass with a Pope she couldn't even see. Michaela laughed at the thought. Her mom was a simple person; she didn't look back on events in a twisted way or view people in a negative light. That simplicity, verging on foolishness, made life more difficult for her. She provided for her husband and served as the head of the family with blind acceptance. When Michaela was in her teens, the relationship of her parents, in which her dad lounged around the house and her mom worked until her hands looked like feet, sometimes struck her as that of a parasite and its host.

Her dad's life was an endless string of finding jobs and losing them. The sickly man had the audacity in his youth to work undercover at a factory while teaching at a night school in order to "dedicate" himself to "the labor movement of this land." He often had heavy nosebleeds during class, and her mom, who was his student at the time, had teared up with boundless pity for him. She would carry the teacher on her back and run around seeking help because he was prone to fainting everywhere, and when they began dating, she would use up all her savings to buy him herbal medicine (*who* was helping *who?*). There was no wedding, no honeymoon. Her dad had been in prison during that period. Her mom's only joy as a new bride was exchanging a few words with him during her weekly visits to prison.

"How thankful I am for those days," she said of that period. She often talked about how every visit had put her in such a good mood starting from the morning before that she ended up spending a sleepless night. The postcards she wrote him each day after work exceeded five hundred.

After her dad was released, referrals by acquaintances got him into a few small companies, but he quit all of them before long. Sometimes, he obtained freelance proofreading or translation jobs from publishers. He didn't earn much money, of course, and fell so ill whenever he finished a book that he had to be hospitalized. To Michaela, her dad was someone who either lay at the hospital getting an IV drip or stirred a bowl of watery porridge with a spoon gripped by skeletal fingers. Despite his frail state, her dad never missed a large protest in Seoul and advised his middle school daughter to read the letters of Kim Dae-jung written from prison and books by Ham Seok-heon.

She thought: What was his problem? What did it matter to our lives whether Kim Dae-jung became president or Lee Hoi-chang did? Her mom, just to pay for her school trip, was perming hair for middle-aged women till her hands looked like feet. Her dad remarked at the dinner table that capital was marginalizing the poor, that the collapse of the middle class would accelerate in the future and plunge more people into poverty.

So what? Dad, the culprit for plunging this family into poverty is not the world, not capital, but you. What right did the man have to say such things when his wife stood all day long at a hair salon hardly 250 square feet because he couldn't earn his own living? But she understood her mom even less. After coming home from work, her mom would get changed and ask about her dad's day. Was he tired today? How was the book he was reading? She thought that her mom's overindulgence had enabled him to dream his pipe dreams without settling down in the world. That her mom was being used by the likes of her dad because she didn't love herself enough. That this wasn't love but one-sided exploitation.

She called her mom. An automated message said the phone was turned off. Her mom had obviously forgotten to bring a charger. Normally, her mom would've called to tell her that her phone was dead. It was strange not to hear at all from someone who would've borrowed another person's phone if necessary to give her a rundown on the Mass and the itinerary for the day. She phoned Scholastica Ajumma.

"I couldn't go to Seoul yesterday. We drew lots and I didn't win, you see. Don't worry about our fellow sister. The old gal always forgets to charge her phone. Hang on, do you have Elizabeth Ajumma's number? Mm-hmm, the lady in the choir."

She dialed Elizabeth Ajumma's number.

"Huh? What do you mean? She said she was sleeping over at your house. Didn't she come by? And she didn't phone, either? Oh dear, what is going on? A girlfriend's place? Does she know anyone in Seoul? Yes, she told us she'll stay with you, I'm sure of it."

While she was on the phone with Elizabeth Ajumma, the television news showed a panorama of Gwanghwamun Square. The camera was filming a booth petitioning for the "Special Act on Investigating the Truth of the April 16 *Sewol* Ferry Disaster and Building a Safe Society." Behind the booth was a tent, in which an old woman and a middle-aged woman sat side by side. It was a fleeting moment, but she knew at once that the middle-aged woman was her mom. The duffel bag lying next to the woman was definitely her mom's, too. But why on earth was her mom sitting there? She ran outside without even washing her face.

4

The jjimjilbang that the woman at the bus stop had told her about was smaller than she expected. She flung off her uncomfortable hanbok and took time to scrub the dirt off her entire body. She spotted mothers and daughters who were visiting the bathhouse together for the long weekend. The sight of children gamboling around like puppies made her chortle. Young mothers sat their children on bath stools, soaping every nook and cranny. The children, too, were making a valiant effort to soap their mothers' backs.

Will I be a grandmother, too, someday? The woman's heart was fit to burst at the thought of a grandchild who might someday run into her arms. Life still opened up and revealed to her a new dream. While the dream had the slimmest chance of coming true, carrying it in her heart seemed to give her new energy and appetite.

Whenever she felt very fortunate to live a particular moment, the woman remembered her husband, who was called to heaven thirteen years ago. Thinking about him, a heavy pendulum seemed to scrape along the bottom of her heart. He never got to see Michaela enter university or watch her grow into a fine young lady. He never saw the Holy Father holding the Mass at Gwang-hwamun, and no . . . he had never been to Jeju Island, either, the vacation spot everyone else in the country appeared to have visited. She often wondered if there ever was a poorer man, yet the thought of his soul resting in a place where he would no longer suffer brought inexplicable tears to her eyes.

The people in the neighborhood pitied the woman for having a husband who couldn't support his family. Michaela told her that she was taking the blow for his incompetence. It was true. Ever since she met him, life demanded two, three times as much submission from her. She lived without a breath to spare and had never even gone to see the pretty autumn leaves like everyone else. She frequented prisons and hospitals where she should've had no business entering, and labored without holidays to fill up their bank account that leaked like a sieve.

But she could not agree with the people who said her husband had made no effort. When it came to his calling, which was to read and write and stay on the scene where he could help, he had applied himself with unparalleled diligence. You couldn't judge him as an incompetent, worthless person just because the work he did made no money.

She believed the world needed a variety of people. Someone who rolled perm rods, yes, but also someone like him. There were husbands who put food on the table, and then there were husbands who did house chores and looked after children. She had never seen, as she made her way in the world, someone as sweet and as delicate as her husband. She could not ask him, a pristine spring, to become dirty bathwater. Yes, he may have looked like a useless person to the world. But not everything that the many useful people in the world did seemed truly useful to the world.

Peeling and eating hard-boiled eggs in the jjimjilbang lounge, the woman observed the twisting veins that bulged in her calves. The cluster of varicose veins almost looked like a green lump. Feeling self-conscious of its shape, she spread a towel over her crossed-legged lap. The swelling had started a little over a year after she became a hairdresser, but with no time to seek treatment, she had neglected it and now it had gotten quite bad. After a tiny, five-year-old customer said, "Mommy, that lady's legs are scary," and burst into tears, she began wearing long pants no matter how hot the day was.

Today's Mass was on the news. Around a million people had gathered, apparently. As her spot had been in Jongno 3-ga, she had not been able to see the Holy Father with her own eyes. Even when he was parading the city in his popemobile, she had been jostled by the crowds and missed him. Some of the taller fellow brothers of her church said they had seen him passing from a distance, but she, a short woman, had seen only an abundance of people's backs and heads.

The Holy Father on the giant screen had often stopped in his tracks, placing a hand on the children's heads to bless them. Then, as he turned a corner, he had spotted a man desperately hailing him and climbed down to the pavement where the man stood. The Holy Father had clasped the man's hands and inclined his head, listening intently to the man speak. The priest by the Holy Father's side had seemed to be interpreting for him. Many people watching this exchange through the screen had cheered. "That's Yoomin's father, one of the *Sewol* disaster parents," fellow sister Susanna had said, the parishioner who sat next to her that day.

The gaunt face of the man speaking so desperately to the Holy Father had stirred a ripple in the woman's heart. Even as she watched the Holy Father depart and resume the parade, the man's face stayed in her mind as if it had been branded there. What had he said to the Holy Father? What could he have said to articulate his undeserved suffering in such a brief moment? What could he have felt as he cried out to the Holy Father to look at him? As he begged someone from the other side of the planet to hear him?

Despite the blessing of celebrating Mass with the Holy Father, despite her great joy, the woman's heart had not been entirely glad. If only she could, she had wanted to push through the crowd to the man and at least give him a hug. That she was powerless to share in his suffering had saddened her. His conversation with the Holy Father was not shown on the news.

While she watched the television, the people lying down in the lounge went out one by one. The food stall lady switched off the fluorescent lights in the stall, then in the restaurant. Due to its small size, the jjimjilbang didn't seem to be the kind where people crowded into the lounge to sit up all night or to sleep. Looking around, she found only three people who had settled down to sleep, all of whom were men: a lad in his thirties, a middle-aged man, and a snowy-haired old man. One of them even turned off the TV at eleven o'clock. She couldn't squeeze in among the men to sleep. And there was no separate sleeping room in the tiny jjimjilbang. She returned to the changing room, covering her calves with a towel.

All that was in the changing room was a U-shaped set of lockers, another row of lockers, and a raised wooden platform. A woman in her sixties was monopolizing the wide platform, drooling copiously as she slept. The floor was warm but the air chilly, perhaps due to the breeze from the air conditioner. She pressed the AC's temperature controls, but the settings seemed to be fixed. She walked over to the U-shaped set of lockers. She was thinking she would have to sleep in the space between the lockers when an old woman who had just finished bathing took the spot and lay down. Giving up, she was about to lie down in the walkway when the old woman came over and offered to sleep in the walkway instead.

"You should sleep inside, my dear. I can sleep anywhere."

The woman declined with a wave of her hand, but, ignoring her, the older woman stretched out in the walkway and pretended to sleep. She squatted next to the old woman and looked into her face. With short white hair and lips pursed from toothlessness, she was hardly five feet tall. As she was nothing but bones, just five minutes on the floor was bound to cause aches all over her body, yet the utter serenity with which she lulled herself to sleep on the bathhouse floor hinted at her history. A veteran knew a veteran when she saw one: this woman must have known no small amount of suffering.

"Ma'am, can you get up?"

The old woman still seemed to be feigning sleep.

"My, she's a tough cookie, this one. Ma'am, you'll be sore all over if you sleep like that. Isn't she cold? And what's wrong with that AC? An old lady's trying to sleep here."

She took out two towels from her duffel bag, which she had

stored in a locker. The white towels were embroidered in blue with the words "Commemorating the Beatification Mass by His Holiness Pope Francis. Ilwol-dong Catholic Church," etc. They were long, wide towels, the kind you might only see in American movies. The church office manager had ordered the wrong size and distributed giant towels to everyone, much to their bewilderment. She had two of the big towels because she was given one by fellow sister Gemma, who said she wouldn't use the thing and it would end up being clutter.

"Ma'am, will you at least sleep on this towel?"

The old woman was still curled up on the bare floor and didn't move a muscle. She covered the old woman's small body with the large towel. Then she walked over to the space between the lockers, pulled the remaining towel over herself, and slept. She, too, knew a thing or two about sleeping anywhere. As she sank into a deep slumber, she recalled the face of the man she had seen at that morning's Mass. *If I were like him and lost my Michaela, how would I go on living* . . . Tears welled up in her eyes just thinking about it. What had he said? She wanted to hear the voice she hadn't been able to hear.

She woke up at the sound of a blow dryer and found a carton of milk on the floor.

"That milk, I left it there for you, my dear. I was buying one for myself and got another."

The old woman, who was very wrinkly around the mouth, was sitting on the platform, beaming.

"That towel of yours was real warm, I must say. You from the Ilwol-dong Church? From so far away? Did you go to the Mass yesterday? But why'd you sleep here instead of going home?"

She rubbed off her eye gunk and walked over to the platform. The old woman looked a good five years younger than she had with her eyes closed, possibly because she was wearing her dentures now.

"My dear, I've met the Holy Father, too, you know. In 1989, at Yeouido. What an honor it was."

"I was there, too!"

She was delighted as though she had met someone she knew. She and the old woman sat on the platform, sharing their memories of that brilliant autumn day in '89. The old woman proposed they grab breakfast together to celebrate this welcome meeting of sisters in Christ, so they went out and headed to a nearby joint that sold bean sprout soup with rice.

She added shrimp paste, hot pepper slices, and even radish kimchi juice to the hot broth; drinking it comforted the stomach and roused the senses. They ate in such a hurry that, until they emptied half of their soup bowls, neither of them explained why they had slept at the jjimjilbang nor told each other their names. Once sufficiently full, she asked the old woman, "So why did you sleep at the jjimjilbang? Are you on your way somewhere?"

"My dear, I, uh . . . don't have too many friends. I didn't have many to begin with 'cause I was never the friendly type, then everybody died over the years and only a couple are still alive." The old woman blew on a spoonful of soup, drank it, and continued, "I have one friend left now that I care about with all my heart. We met well into our sixties, and she's not like me at all. I'm the cranky, prickly sort, but she is mighty easygoing. Whatever happens, she laughs it off, bless her. She's a lovely soul. Never speaks ill of nobody. I met her at my granddaughter's playground, soon after I moved to the neighborhood. We were raising granddaughters around the same age, you see. Turns out, we went to the same church. That's how we became close. We'd both lost our husbands and were living with our children. We met every day. Talking about our lives, our sorrows. And you know what? She listened to my stories and cried with me. I've never met anyone quite like her. My son's family moved to Seoul, but I stayed back in that neighborhood and lived on my own. She became a sister to me. She brought her granddaughter with her everywhere 'cause her daughter and son-in-law both worked. Oh, how she doted on her only grandkid, and what a sweet lovely girl she was, too, just like her grandmother. When the child saw me in the churchyard, she'd give me a jolly greeting, press cookies into my hands, and ask if I was eating well, that's what she was like . . ." The old woman broke off and suddenly wailed like a child. A few grains of rice dribbled out of her mouth. People stared mutely at this old woman who was wailing in a hangover soup joint so early in the morning. She cried for a while like that, then she wiped her tears, blew her nose, and drank some water.

"I thought I'd already shed all the tears I had to shed in all my eighty years. How wrong I was. Wrong. She, my lovely friend, was out of her poor mind, trying to rip her heart out, but there was nothing I could do for her. She'd lost a perfectly healthy grandkid, just like that—how could anyone possibly bear such a thing? After watching the child's final moments, my friend's daughter threw away her work and started running around everywhere. Had to find out why her daughter died, didn't she? My friend joined her daughter and went to Gwanghwamun, to City Hall, to Yeouido. It's hard to get a hold of her. Yesterday I went to Gwanghwamun again to find her, but then the buses stopped running, that's why I went to the jjimjilbang."

When the old woman finished speaking, both women were crying.

"I'm going to look for her today, too."

5

Her mom's cell phone was still turned off. She got on a bus bound for Gwanghwamun and thought back to the woman she had just seen on TV. The woman had been wearing navy linen pants that had bled most of their color and a cherry-pink polo shirt, which she had given to her mom for her last birthday. Even that wispy, permed hair dyed brown. The woman on TV was definitely her mom. What in the world was her mom doing there? She was speechless at her mom's infinite capacity to meddle in other people's business.

She got off at Gwanghwamun Station and made to cross the street when she spotted a group of people standing in the scorching sun, a sign hung around each of their necks reading, I AM JOINING THE ONE-DAY HUNGER STRIKE. One man in his forties, and two women who looked to be in their early twenties. The man, who had stuck to his back a written plea to investigate the truth behind the *Sewol* ferry sinking, was staring at passersby. The two girls were handing out pamphlets to people, but she dodged around them and crossed the street.

There were many people signing the petition at the square. She had also signed it on her way to Kyobo Bookstore a few months ago. Nearly four months had passed since the sinking, but the facts of what happened that day hadn't even been established yet, and the victims' families were demanding that the government legislate the Sewol Ferry Act, which would endow investigation and indictment powers to an independent commission. When opposition lawmakers suddenly sang a different tune and announced the compromise they had reached with the governing party, a compromise that excluded the victims' families and their demands, she had switched off the television.

That was how it was. For all the signature collections and street protests, it seemed that those voices were more and more confined to the minority. Too quickly, the world forgot what had happened and brushed it under the rug. When at lunch someone spoke about the necessity of the Sewol Ferry Act then fell silent after being told "Not that again," she bit her lip. She was thirty-one, and though her peers had banded together they failed to effect a single change. The world seemed impenetrable, as though hurling all of herself against it would not even leave a hairline crack. Her twenties had taught her that knowing what was wrong didn't mean you could change it.

Her dad once said that what ruined the world was the apathy of the good-hearted majority. He was right, but she didn't want to fight a world like that. She didn't want to step into a boxing ring that guaranteed defeat. To her, the world was a place she had to bow down to even if she didn't like it, a place she had to adapt to even if that meant marginalizing or modifying herself. Instead of clashing with it, she wanted to be incorporated into it. She wanted the world to invite her in.

She usually sped up when passing through Gwanghwamun, but today she couldn't do that. Walking around the square slowly, she stared about in search of the tent she had seen on the news. To her surprise, many of the people collecting signatures or giving out pamphlets were young. She resigned herself to being handed a pamphlet but said she had signed the petition a while back.

Suddenly, she wondered when this struggle would end. Public opinion was growing less sympathetic by the day. The *victims* would look bad if the fight dragged on. They would be charged with the crime of not acquiescing to the state, added to the offense of raising a needless fuss. Hadn't the president even said so? That we must forget the past and move into the future now? She could barely open her eyes in the stinging sunlight.

A woman stood in front of a tent wearing navy pants and a cherry-pink shirt. She put a hand on the woman's shoulder.

"Mom."

But the woman who looked around was not her mom.

"Who are you?" she asked the woman.

"Miss, my daughter was also on the ferry that day," said the woman. Apart from her face, the woman resembled her mom in every respect. The navy pants had bled out precisely the same amount of color, and the cherry-pink shirt was of the same brand and design. The beige sandals, the duffel bag lying nearby, the rosary ring on the woman's right index finger, the rosary bracelet around the left wrist were all identical to her mom's. The woman even had the same Big Dipper–shaped moles on her neck and the same scar on her forehead. Even that low, gentle voice sounded just like her mom's.

"Please don't forget my daughter. You mustn't forget her."

The woman said that and moved on to the other people passing the square. She stood rooted to the spot as if she had been struck. A group of tourists followed their guide to the statue of Admiral Yi Sun-sin. Listening to their loud burst of laughter, she searched for the woman who had blended into the crowd.

My daughter was also on the ferry that day. That voice had definitely been her mom's.

The voice cut deep into her heart.

6

The woman got on a Gwanghwamun-bound bus with the old woman. Scenes of Seoul she saw out the bus window struck her as beautiful. Young couples and children on their Sunday outings, young women striding past exposing their white, smooth legs—how lively and pretty they all looked. Every street teemed with beautiful, handsome people who could've walked straight out of the television. She thought of her daughter, Michaela, who was prettier than anyone she knew. She had really wanted to see Michaela but had a feeling she would not get to.

The woman often dabbed tears from her eyes ever since the incident. Chatting with the salon customers, doing her groceries, thinking of her daughter who lived in Seoul, she wept in silence. Her heart smarted and stung as though it had been scorched by fire. She thought of the innumerable days those people could have lived. Even though their lives could've been saved and there had been enough time to do so, even though everyone could've survived, we had, like a lie, lost them before our very eyes.

Guilt plagued her. Even her own pity distressed her because she didn't want to pity them as a way to shake off that deep, deep guilt. Easter arrived not long after the incident. She could not spend Easter Week, her favorite time of the year, as she normally did. The joyful message of Christ's resurrection did not reach her heart; it only drifted far away. Even the greeting "Rejoice, fellow sister, it is Easter" felt like an act of violence that obstructed her from mourning them. For the first time in her life, she could not attend Easter Mass.

As always, time passed and the heart's pain dulled. The customers who used to be furious and tearful over the matter stopped mentioning it, while some customers even complained of their fatigue with the people who couldn't forget it quickly enough. Listening to their words wounded her all over again. She shut her mouth, rolled her perm rods, gave them haircuts, served them coffee. Truly, she did not wish to hate anyone.

She glanced at the old woman who sat dozing off beside her. How many times had this old woman lost her loved ones? She felt a certain respect for every elderly person she saw. Because to live a long life was to see your loved ones go before you and get left behind for a long time, to suffer that ordeal then once again stand up and eat and walk your path alone.

A piece of her had died with the deaths of her parents and husband, vanishing from the world along with the departed. For a while she could not breathe or sleep or eat properly. After many sleepless nights and long bouts of crying, all that remained was a life without them and the world they had left her. All of it dear. She wanted to show them, who were still alive inside her, a better world and a better her. She wanted her heart, now cleansed from grief, to mirror only sweet and beautiful things for them to see.

She woke the old woman snoozing on her shoulder and got off the bus. Chinese tourists were walking toward Gwanghwamun Square in droves. Grubby yellow ribbons, tied to clotheslines strung between trees, fluttered in the wind. Several young people were collecting petition signatures. It was a hot day. She took out a water bottle from her duffel bag and handed it to the old woman, then took a swig herself. The old woman, who had a hunched back, took five steps and rested awhile, then took another five steps and rested awhile. She was worried about the old woman's state.

"I'm sorry, my dear. Normally I can walk fine, but I'm in a bad way today."

"Easy does it. We're not in a race, are we?"

"All this trouble, dear, because of me, when you're here to see Seoul."

They were standing before a crosswalk when two young women approached, a sign hung around each of their necks reading, PETITION TO PASS SEWOL FERRY ACT. One of them was holding pamphlets and the other a pen with a file of signature sheets. Both of their faces were flushed from the sun. They helped the old woman across the crosswalk.

"Thank you," the woman said after they had all crossed.

"Please give this pamphlet a read. Have you signed yet?"

The old woman nodded and the woman signed the sheet she was handed.

"We're looking for someone. An elderly lady named Kim Ip

Boon. She's a friend of this lady here. What was her daughter's name again?" asked the woman.

"Lee Myungsoon. Lee Myungsoon Maria," replied the old woman.

"Ms. Lee Myungsoon is a surviving family member," said the woman.

"I wouldn't know her just by her name. Was the victim a student by any chance?"

"Yes."

"May I know the student's name then? We normally use the student's name and call family members 'so-and-so's mother' or 'so-and-so's father.'"

The old woman closed her eyes, then said, "I can't really remember her name. I just called her Michaela from when she was little. She's never been called by her name since she was a small tyke. Her grandmother just called her Michaela, too. My friend would even call 'Michaela, dear' when she was sitting by herself."

Quietly, the woman watched the old woman's lips enunciate "Michaela."

Michaela was a common baptismal name for girls.

The woman had become pregnant with her current daughter after three missed miscarriages.

"I will pray to the angel Michaela for you."

A salon customer whose face she couldn't remember now had told her so, with assurances that the angel Michaela, vanquisher of all darkness in the world, would protect the tiny life that had taken root inside her. Her daughter descended safely on the world eight months later, and she called the newborn Michaela. Though Soojin was the child's name, she preferred to call her Michaela; she believed the name would protect the child.

With the birth of her daughter, light flooded into the woman's shadowed heart. Even its coldest corners thawed when her little girl toddled over them. The embankments and fences she had painstakingly built up crumbled with one touch of her daughter's hands, the child's laughter a rain flowing into dried-up streams. She gave the child all that was and wasn't in her heart without worrying or fearing that her heart would not return to her. She was simply in that heart, warm.

The child protected the woman through her own breath, her own light. She kept her mother safe from the whispers of the world's darkness. All children, the woman thought, were angels who guarded their parents' lives. Nobody had the right to snatch those angels away from the arms of their parents. Nobody.

The woman held the old woman by the arm as they made their way across the square in search of Michaela's mother and grandmother. And she hoped that the path lying ahead of them would not prove too long and arduous. That the world, so calm after savagely trampling on wounded hearts, would cause them no further hurt.

"Mom!" Michaela called the woman. The woman wiped her flowing tears and called her little girl through her heart.

Michaela.

The Secret

1

Malja read the store signs out loud in her head. Two Thousand Two Eyeglasses, Famous Original Grilled Octopus, Odari Marinated Crab Restaurant, Lee Eunmi's Oriental Clinic, DS Print... Although she went down this street at least once every six months, it somehow looked different each time. It was already her eighth year of traveling this street in her daughter's car. Some days she laughed, on others she cried, and on still others she was struck dumb. And at all such moments, she read the words on the street that she saw out the car window.

According to her doctor, Malja should've died seven years ago. The doctor had told her she had six months to live, or at most a year to a year and a half. Her reaction ran the gamut from howling in disbelief at her own fate to envying all healthy people who lived without staying conscious of death. Fortunately, her surgery and chemotherapy went well. She did everything her doctor told her to do. She got up at six in the morning, ate a breakfast of brown rice and mostly vegetables, and walked for two hours. Every day, she drank water infused with shiitake mushrooms and ate steamed sweet potatoes with the skin on. Telling herself she would die if she starved, she force-fed herself through violent retching. She slept, awoke, ate, and exercised with religious punctuality.

Five years later, Malja's cancer was declared to have gone into complete remission. The person most thrilled by the news was her granddaughter, Jimin, who buried her head in Malja's skirt and sobbed like she used to as a baby. Jimin hadn't once shown tears during the chemotherapy; Malja finally understood how much the child had been suffering. Six months later, the cancer cells began to spread again, and the situation kept worsening. Today, Malja once again received gloomy test results from the doctor.

Malja was troubled that her daughter Youngsook, who was driving, looked so wan. She wanted to ask, "Are you sick?" but kept the question to herself as she knew Youngsook would only snap back, "*You're* seriously asking me that?" Youngsook was drying the tears streaming down her cheeks with the back of her hand as she drove. Malja knew it was best to say nothing at such times. For the last eight years her daughter had suffered on her account, and Malja had no idea how she could ever make it up to her. She was always at a loss for words before Youngsook, who, because she was born to *her* of all people, had endured every possible hardship.

Youngsook seemed to have turned into a completely different person over the last year and a half. She had visibly lost weight and her speech was often confused over the phone. She, who had hardly called once a week, now called nonstop to rant about her husband, her coworkers, and her clients. Malja was worried for Youngsook, this unfamiliar person spewing poisonous words mixed with the foulest insults. Sometimes, Youngsook phoned at night, drunk, and cried, "Mom! Mom!" then sobbed the whole time. Malja could only repeat her daughter's name—"Youngsook, oh, Youngsook"—and did not know what else to say. After these phone sessions, she would feel her daughter's emotions so acutely that the pit of her stomach clenched and her forehead broke out in a sweat. Later when she asked, "Why'd you cry so much on the phone the other day?" Youngsook would give her dubious excuses: "Mom, I can't remember anything. I must have a bad case of menopause."

Come to think of it, it had also been a year and a half since Jimin left for China.

Malja lived two hours away from her daughter by intercity bus. She used to live with her daughter's family but moved out when Jimin's dad got a job in Seoul. Jimin was in grade nine and no longer needed her grandmother to look after her. Malja had raised Jimin at the request of her daughter and son-in-law, who both worked outside the house. Parting with Jimin, from whom she had been inseparable since the child was an infant, was like cutting out her own flesh, but she didn't want to be a burden to her daughter's family by following them to Seoul, especially when they were moving to a smaller house. On the morning of the move, Jimin brought out a sheet of newspaper and nail clippers and sat in front of Malja, who clipped Jimin's fingernails and toenails with more care than she had ever taken.

"You've got long, slender hands, so you'll live a pretty life. An' not have it rough like yer granny did."

"Here we go again."

"Yer gonna be a teacher, Jimin. You'll teach students."

Malja remembered wanting to say more but being too choked up to continue. Her vision blurred and she couldn't make out those dainty hands of Jimin's. Seeing Malja lose her grip, Jimin also began crying. It was a sad memory yet also a happy one in retrospect. Malja missed Jimin every day from then on. She called out the child's name in her sleep and searched for her face whenever she saw groups of students around her age walking by in school uniforms. Now and then when she and Jimin arranged to meet, she couldn't sleep a wink the night before.

Malja had coddled Jimin. She fed her baby food she'd made herself with ground beef, and bought pretty fabric and worked the sewing machine to dress her in clothes that no one else had. She showered Jimin with love lest this only child of working parents should ever feel lonely. She had not been able to do the same for her own daughter, Youngsook.

Youngsook lost her dad when she was five. Malja left the pretty thing, calling "Mommy, Mommy," at her sister-in-law's house to take up a job at a restaurant. It had constantly pained Malja to watch her little tyke growing wise beyond her years, always playing the part of an adult. This was why Malja wanted to bring up Jimin as a very immature child. She wanted her to be a fussy, spoiled brat who couldn't even clip her own nails.

Jimin started school, where she learned to write her name in Hangul and the Chinese characters for one, two, three, four, and five. Malja neatly sharpened pencils for her granddaughter, who practiced her writing in large letters in a grid notebook. Once she mastered the Hangul alphabet, Jimin read any and every word she laid eyes on. Samho Townhouse! Joongang Kindergarten! One-way street! Workers wanted! What a pleasure it was to watch the child twitter in the delight of reading.

The day Jimin received full marks on a dictation test for the first time, Malja went boasting around the market, clutching the test paper in one hand and Jimin's hand in the other.

"Look here. This is my granddaughter, look at her test paper."

"Oh my, you've got a granddaughter to be proud of."

"Mind you, she's always been clever. I'm not sayin' that just 'cause she's my grandkid."

Unprompted, Malja showed off her granddaughter's score to everyone at the fruit and vegetable store, then the fish store, then the dried seafood store. The shoe store was no exception. She had stopped by to get Jimin a pretty pair of sneakers, but her boasts ended in an unnecessary fight.

"Big deal, Mrs. Cho. It's not even a real test. If you brag about full marks on a simple dictation quiz, people will scoff, you know."

"If this ain't a real test, what is it then?"

"Alright, alright. I'm sure *you* would think that."

"Now what's that supposed to mean, Mrs. Kim? What do you mean *I* would think that?"

"I get that you're all impressed since you don't know your alphabet, but what's so amazing about spelling?"

"*Excuse me*, Mrs. Kim?"

After a round of heated bickering, Malja pulled on Jimin's hand and led her out of the market. The shoe store woman had a knack for riling people up with the most innocent look on that dainty face of hers. Often, she proudly displayed a photograph of herself in a white blouse and black flared skirt, saying she'd been a high school graduate back in the day. Malja feigned disinterest, but as someone who'd never so much as crossed the threshold of a school, she was green with envy on every such occasion. Neighborhood women talking about their school days made her feel left out, as if they were excluding just her on purpose, and stung her with unnecessary feelings of inferiority.

Malja had heard of cram schools in big cities that taught Hangul to adults, but for her, a small-towner, such classes were like rice cakes in a painting to a starving person.

Jimin held out a sheet of laminated paper that evening.

"Take a look at this, Grandma."

"What's this?"

"If you learn this, you can read everything like I can."

"That so?"

Malja stared at the laminated paper Jimin was holding. It looked like a jumble of confusing pictures.

"Practice with me for just ten nights, Grandma."

Jimin pointed a small finger at one of the drawings and said, "This is 'ㅏ.' Repeat after me, Grandma. Ah."

Malja said "eeh" when Jimin said "eeh," "oh" when she said "oh." It was a curious business even when she looked back on it now. A mere eight-year-old sitting an adult down to teach her Gah, Nah, Dah, Rah. Jimin gave excellent explanations that Malja could instantly understand. She didn't embarrass Malja for getting something wrong or rush her for not grasping something right away. Whatever Malja got wrong Jimin took note of and asked about later, and for whatever Malja got right she offered praise. Just as Jimin had promised, Malja was able to read every Hangul character on the laminated sheet after ten nights, and with more time she could read, though stumblingly, the words in newspapers and advertisements. A true wireless phone should bend! Maxon Electronics. Thirty House, the twenty-four-hour convenience store. Call for franchise partners!

The world was full of letters. Meaningless pictures turned into words that now spoke to her. She read school newsletters and checked field trip dates, feeling pleased with herself. She wrote her name, "Cho Malja," on the cover of a grid notebook and did homework together with Jimin. She didn't know how to thank Jimin enough.

Malja still remembered how much she had wanted to go to school at Jimin's age. Once, when she wheedled her big brother into sneaking her inside his classroom, his homeroom teacher had pulled up a chair for her. What's your name? The teacher's inquiring voice and gaze had been kind. Cho Malja, she had replied, and hung her head in embarrassment, but the teacher gave her a sheet of newsprint and pencil and asked her to draw. The teacher smelled of a pleasant fragrance she had never smelled before. *Maybe she's a sky-fairy like from the stories.* Even now at seventy, Malja still remembered the fair-skinned teacher in her nice clothes playing the reed organ. She remembered the feeling that had come over her then, of her body growing soft and light as if she were riding a cloud, and she remembered the puppy, the walnut tree, the house, and the fences she had drawn on the newsprint.

Malja's mother slapped her as soon as she returned home. Because she, a girl, didn't know her place and had dared to look around a school. The May sun was scorching. Malja squatted in one of the long furrows of the cabbage field, sniveling, then she swallowed her tears. She never set foot near a school again. If she had occasion to pass by one, she avoided it by taking detours no matter how long they were. But she couldn't tell all of that history to Jimin. She couldn't tell her, You were my first teacher, you were the first person to praise me warmly.

2

Her daughter spread out a blanket on the living room floor and fell asleep snoring as soon as her head touched the blanket. Malja gazed quietly at Youngsook's sleeping face. Dense white strands lined her scalp, rendering her dyed black hair useless, and the crown of her head was disconcertingly bald. As a young woman, Youngsook had boasted tresses so thick that her elastic became taut after just wrapping it twice. Youngsook had been sick in every part of her body since turning thirty, having suffered many hardships in her youth and gone back to work without proper postnatal care.

Son-in-law Park was the eldest son of three from a family of only sons. His mother had kicked up a storm when Youngsook couldn't get pregnant after she had Jimin. The woman phoned Youngsook on every whim and came down on her ruthlessly. As Malja lived in her son-in-law's house, she didn't feel comfortable starting a fight with his mother. Given her usual temper, she would've liked to flatten the woman's nose, but she had to hold herself back for Youngsook's sake. Even when the woman sometimes drove her crazy with snide remarks, the only thing she could say was, Yes, yes, Mrs. Park, and mollify her.

At thirty-two, Youngsook had to undergo a hysterectomy.

"You've cut off this family's bloodline."

Youngsook had been lying in the hospital ward after her big surgery when her mother-in-law attacked her, heedless of what should or shouldn't be said.

"Daughter-in-laws of other families bear two or three sons just fine. Just our luck to have a thing like you join this family."

If she had her way, Malja would've liked to knock the woman down in an all-out, let's-murder-each-other frenzy, but instead she said nothing. She believed that as the wife's mother, she had to stay quiet for her daughter's sake, for the sake of Youngsook's peaceful marriage. Malja walked up to Youngsook's mother-in-law to calm the fuming woman then found Jimin crouching right next to her.

"How long you been sittin' here?"

Jimin did not look up at Malja.

"Sweetie, how long you been here?"

Jimin was crying with her head down. Malja thought her whole head might burst into flames from rage. How could anyone say such trash in the presence of a child? Before that moment, Malja had never sided with Youngsook out of respect for her mother-in-law and had always told her to be good to her husband's mother, thinking that was how a wise mother should act. But had she been wise to stay silent when her daughter had suffered such humiliations? Hadn't her failure to protect her daughter ended up wounding her precious granddaughter now, too?

"Mrs. Park, I suggest you leave it at that. Don't you see the child's a-cryin'?" Though Malja tried to keep her words polite, she could not hide the tremble in her voice. "Cut off yer family's bloodline? Did yer granddaughter here drop from the sky? As for me, I would never trade my Jimin with ten grandsons, Mrs. Park."

"Have you no shame, raising your voice at me!"

"Is it a sin to take out yer uterus 'cause yer sick? Watch yer mouth in the presence of a patient. Even an ignorant crone like me has been taught that much."

There were many more things Malja wanted to say, but her tongue had suddenly stiffened. How dare this woman break her baby's heart and say such filth within her grandkid's earshot? Unsure what might come tumbling out of her mouth if she stayed any longer, Malja grabbed Jimin's wrist and dragged her out to the hospital corridor. Her granddaughter's small hand was cold and damp. Malja couldn't bring herself to look at the child's face as she took her to the convenience store on the hospital's ground floor.

"What do you feel like a-havin'? You name it, Granny'll buy it. Would you like Bong Bong juice or Sac Sac juice?"

Malja walked out of the hospital holding Jimin's hand. She always took Jimin on a stroll when the child cried. Fresh air and a change of scenery, she knew, abated sorrow. She didn't want the child to know sorrow. How she hoped that Jimin wouldn't have to cry over things she didn't need to waste tears on, or feel pain that didn't need to be felt. That she would be free from life's constant intrusions and bullying. Jimin had to be someone who welcomed and savored life, not someone who endured it.

"Jimin honey, don't you take it to heart."

Jimin, who had stopped crying at some point, leaned on Malja's arm.

"By the time you grow up, whether yer a man or woman won't matter no more. If someone tells you you can't 'cause yer a woman, brush it off as ignorant nonsense an' laugh in their face. You can be anyone an' you can do anythin'. In yer generation, a person who has their heart in the right place will always be well off, man or woman."

Youngsook's mother-in-law was gone by the time Malja returned to the ward. Malja drew nearer to her daughter, who lay on the bed, her face swollen. When she saw Malja, she smiled with a furrowed brow. Malja stroked her forehead again and again until she fell asleep. Jimin sat on the trundle bed, quietly watching her mother and grandmother.

3

Malja went into Jimin's room while Youngsook slept.

The room looked just as it did when the child left for China. Everything was sparkling clean thanks to her tidy father, who swept and wiped down the room daily. The five-tier shelf was packed with books and the ones Jimin had studied for her exam still lay on the desk. Malja sat on Jimin's desk chair, peering at the notes and photographs Jimin had stuck to the wall. Handwritten notes faded from sunlight read, "The darkest hour is just before dawn," or "No crazy, no gain," or "Get it together, Jimin." There was also a photograph of Jimin with her students during her teaching practicum. She was standing behind a podium, surrounded by children who were making hearts with their hands. Her smile was so wide that her already small eyes were barely visible.

Jimin once said she had considered working for a standard corporation but decided to become a teacher after doing her practicum. "Grandma, I love kids. They give me life." Malja remembered Jimin's face and the sparkle in her eyes when she said that. Next to the photograph was another one of her with her students at the first school she was assigned to. Jimin, smiling and flashing a V sign with the children in front of a cherry blossom tree. The children, who had linked arms with Jimin, also looked happy.

Malja examined the pictures sandwiched between the desk and its glass cover. Most of them had been taken at school with students. There was also a letter signed by many students on pink cartridge paper. "You're my favorite teacher, Ms. Jimin." "You're so funny, Ms. Jimin. I sleep through all the other classes but not in yours. Do I get brownie points, Teach?" "Ms. Jimin, thx for getting me pastry at the snack bar the other day. I'll gear up and slay the next exams." "We love you, Ms. Jimin a.k.a. Anpanman, LOL."

The kids had drawn Jimin's face in a cartoony style. Once, when Malja asked, "What's Anpanman?," Jimin had searched the image on her phone and shown it to her, laughing. A man with a bun for a face was flying across the sky wearing a cape. "My goodness, how in the world do you look like this baldy?" Malja had burst out furiously, making Jimin dissolve into laughter. With a pang, Malja found herself sorely missing the days she and Jimin had talked about such things in this very room.

There were pictures of Jimin with Malja, too. One was taken at the front gate of Jimin's kindergarten on her first day there. Dressed in a new wool coat and white tights, Jimin was picking her nose. Malja looked like she was telling her something, probably along the lines of "You'll get a nosebleed if you keep on pickin' yer nose." So much time had passed since then, and now Malja was seventy and Jimin twenty-eight. Jimin, who used to be glued to Malja every day like a part of her body, hadn't once been in touch after going away to distant lands.

Even though time had changed everything, Malja felt she could almost reach into and touch that scene in the photograph. Everything felt like yesterday: washing the child, dressing her in thermals, combing her hair, pulling socks over her little feet, running after her when she broke into a run lest she trip and scrape her knees yet again, tucking in a sleepy-cranky Jimin and patting her to sleep while Malja herself inadvertently dozed off.

Another picture was from their trip to Jeju Island two years ago in fall. Jimin, Youngsook, and Malja had gone on a four-day trip to celebrate Malja's complete remission. They went horseback riding, visited the Teddy Bear Museum, and saw no less than two giant waterfalls. They ate black pork belly, peanut ice cream, and Omegi rice cake. Youngsook had driven and Jimin had done the research for accommodations, restaurants, and attractions beforehand, so Malja had only to go along for the ride.

The photograph had been taken on a white sandy beach of Udo. It was Malja's first time seeing white sands and sky-colored water. Jimin told her the white sand was formed from broken coral. Malja said she wanted to dip her feet in the water, at which Jimin pulled off her own socks and waded into the sea first. Both of them were ankle-deep in the water, laughing, when Youngsook snapped a picture of them.

Malja had felt her chest tighten as she watched Jimin chatter-
ing away, arm in arm with her. On the ferry from Udo to Seongsan Port, Malja had gazed at Jimin for a while then said:

"Jimin?"

"Mm-hmm?"

"This is the last time."

"For what?"

"Y'know, the last time you take me around."

"What're you talking about, Grandma?"

"If you've got time an' money, spend 'em on what's good for *you*."

"Grandma."

"Mm-hmm."

"When I become a real teacher, I'll take you around to see
more wonderful things."

"What are ya if not a real teacher? You mean to say there's fake
teachers in the world?"

"I'm still a probationary teacher."

"What's probansionary?"

At this Jimin had written "probationary teacher" on a tissue
with a pen.

"I didn't pass the exam that makes you a teacher yet."

Malja had stared hard at the words "probationary teacher."
She'd failed to make sense of the term no matter how long she
stared, but had just nodded, pretending to have understood. A
teacher was a teacher; she couldn't see why this probansionary or
probationary business had to be so complicated.

Sitting at Jimin's desk, Malja pictured again the scene aboard the ferry to Seongsan Port. She saw Jimin's long hair flailing about in the strong wind, her small, chubby hand brushing back the strands stuck to her face. Though Jimin called herself a grown-up, in Malja's eyes she was still a child left unattended around dangerous waters. Someday I will have to leave you, but I'm not worried, Malja had thought as she stood on the deck. There will be tough moments, but you of all people will overcome them, you will enjoy your share of happiness. Back then, Malja had believed that. Watching Jimin's pristine face smiling her clear smile, Malja had truly believed that.

4

Son-in-law Park's face had grown noticeably gaunt since Malja had seen him some time ago. Absently looking into his mouth when he yawned, she glimpsed a few gaping holes where there should have been molars.

"Son-in-law Park, am I seein' things or did ya lose a few teeth?"

He wasn't giving her much of an answer when Youngsook interjected, "He's just getting old."

"Son-in-law Park—"

"Mother-in-law, is this really the time for you to worry about me? Please, just worry about yourself!"

Son-in-law Park had a tendency to lose his temper. Normally you lose your temper when you're angry, but he also lost his temper when he was embarrassed or happy or surprised. In the early days of living with her son-in-law, Malja had jumped out of her skin every time he had one of his outbursts, but now she was used to them. He would shout for no reason, go smoke a cigarette, then come back and furtively try to read the three women's moods. A tall, bulky man with intimidating features, he often gave people the wrong impression.

As he went out holding a cigarette, his retreating figure didn't seem what it once was. Not only had his waist and thighs grown so skinny that this pants looked too big, but his body seemed to have shrunk overall. Malja's heart hurt to see how frail he had become in so short a time.

Once, Malja had come back from the hospital and was sleeping in Jimin's room when she heard the front door open and something drop to the floor with a thud. Startled, she went outside to find her son-in-law, drunk as a lord, sprawled in the entryway without even taking off his shoes. Her son-in-law was rarely a sloppy drunk. She tried to calm her nerves as she watched him flounder on the floor unable to coordinate his limbs.

"Youngsook, Youngsook!" He hollered the name, then began to weep quietly.

"Honey. If you're going to cry, cry loudly, you foolish man. Just cry all you want when you're with me. Why do you have to walk on eggshells even around me?"

Youngsook pounded her husband's back with her fists again and again. Malja went back into her room, embarrassed that she had intruded on their private moment. She lay down only after she heard Youngsook taking Son-in-law Park into the bedroom, but she found it hard to fall asleep.

"Jimin went to China. She's going to teach in the countryside there." Son-in-law Park's flushed face when he said those words flickered before Malja's eyes as she lay awake.

On Jimin's birthday, Malja made japchae and took it to her daughter's place. Beef seaweed soup, japchae, spicy cockles, shredded radish salad, and Jimin's other favorite dishes were laid out on the table. On Jimin's birthday last year, Youngsook had said she and her husband were going on a trip somewhere. She explained they had decided not to prepare a feast since the birthday girl wasn't present anyway.

Once everyone was gathered around the birthday table, it all felt rather pointless. All three of them said nothing as if by agreement, and Son-in-law Park only had a few spoonfuls of soup before withdrawing into the bedroom. Malja looked at Youngsook, who had mixed rice into her soup and was stuffing it down her throat.

"Do you want more soup? To wash the rice down?"

Youngsook continued to eat without looking up from her soup bowl but choked, spraying bits of rice over the table.

"Sorry, Mom," Youngsook said, flustered, as she cleaned the rice off the table. I'm sorry, I'm sorry, Mom.

What was she so sorry about? Malja was annoyed at her daughter apologizing over every little thing. Malja was going to say she needed to chew her food slowly, but the words wouldn't come out. Youngsook, she wanted to say at least, but even calling out her name was difficult. Instead, Malja poured more soup into Youngsook's bowl. Youngsook began to eat the rice again, slowly this time, blowing on the soup. Malja also chewed the soft seaweed stems as slowly as she could before swallowing.

Once she'd finished eating, Youngsook said she would step out for a bit to buy bread. She did not return even after Malja had done the dishes, folded the laundry, and vacuumed. Malja sat on the couch watching television for about an hour before going home. The autumn rain, falling tactlessly on Jimin's birthday, was cold. The thought that Youngsook might be walking around in this cold rain weighed down on each step Malja took toward the bus terminal. When she phoned after getting home, Youngsook didn't pick up.

There was no word from Jimin for nearly half a year after she moved to China. She had apparently left in such a hurry that she couldn't even say goodbye to Malja. It was around this time that Youngsook called to share news of Jimin. Youngsook said she had finally managed to reach Jimin by phone.

"Mom, Jimin says she's living in a mountain valley. So she can't phone or write."

Malja was silent.

"China is so huge, Mom, that apparently there are areas in the countryside where mail carriers can't even access."

"Yes, China's huge."

"Her school sounds extremely busy, too. It doesn't have holidays."

"I see."

"So she wanted me to tell you not to worry, she's doing fine . . ."

"I'm sure she's fine."

Youngsook was silent.

"You bet, our Jimin is doin' just fine."

5

Malja opened Jimin's wardrobe. She saw a winter coat, a jacket for spring and fall, several blazers Jimin used to wear to work, a cardigan, a suit skirt, and next to that some summer dresses. Because the clothes were packed together in the small wardrobe, two summer dresses came sliding off their hangers when Malja took out a cardigan. The cardigan was dark gray with three buttons down the front. Jimin had worn it all the time even though the material wasn't very warm and was pilling heavily. Malja had told her many times to throw it out, but Jimin wouldn't hear of it.

An old, heavy piece of clothing made of cheap synthetic fiber.

Malja held it up and hugged it as though it were a person. Since Jimin wasn't home, this was a good opportunity to chuck the hideous thing, but Malja couldn't do it. She felt that Jimin, when she came back someday, would interrogate her on the cardigan's whereabouts. Malja sometimes tried on Jimin's favorite clothes in secret after her daughter and son-in-law had gone to bed. She mostly wore them just inside the room, but when she felt like it, she would go out and about in those clothes or take some home to hug while she slept.

Malja put on Jimin's cardigan and observed her reflection in the wardrobe mirror. An old woman, skinny as a skewer, was standing hunched over. Her sunken eyes and lack of eyebrows made it seem she had a cryptic expression on her face even though she was simply staring. Malja was seeing her reflection in the mirror for the first time in quite a bit. Ever since she began to lose weight, she hadn't looked straight into a mirror because she dreaded seeing her face. She took out Jimin's beige scarf and draped it around her neck. Though she had only put on Jimin's clothes and scarf, her body was drained of strength and her legs shook. She lay down on Jimin's bed.

The doctor had cautiously told her that even with surgery, there wasn't much hope. Once upon a time such words would've broken her, but now she felt at peace. She was done with surgery, and with chemotherapy. There was nothing to prolong her life for, nor did she have any regrets. It was just as well. Not that she didn't fear death, but staying alive was just as scary and, in that sense, no different from dying. She didn't know how to arrange her face in front of Youngsook when she was hiding these feelings. She tossed and turned on the bed. She couldn't sleep.

Grandma.

Ever since Jimin went away to that place, Malja heard Jimin's voice in her head many times. It always said "Grandma" and nothing else. That voice and that word were what she longed to hear more than anything else in all the world. But over time she couldn't hear Jimin's voice anymore. Now she couldn't even remember the child's voice exactly. How could she not remember Jimin's voice—from what devilry? It felt like punishment. So whenever Jimin's voice faded or when the child seemed to drift away from her, Malja would carefully sharpen a pencil and write a letter to her.

Malja got up and went to Jimin's desk.

Jimin,

Are you doing well there? Are you teaching the children well there, too? Don't you worry about us. We're all doing fine.

Do you know, you used to cry so much as a tot. I have never seen a bigger crybaby than you in all my years. Having to look after my daughter's kid in my old age felt unfair at first. Whenever you bawled your head off, why, I wondered what I'd done so wrong to deserve taking you on.

How long the nights were with you mewling away, Jimin dear. I wasn't like other folks who are fond of children. But how did I end up the way I am now? I ain't got an explanation if anyone asks.

Granny was scared of liking people, Jimin. It hurts to like someone and it's hard. Maybe because Granny is a chicken but I started dreading that kinda thing at some point. Still, I thought I'd grow out of it later. But I didn't, did I? Turns out that even when my eyes grew old and my ears grew old and my hands and feet hardened like tree bark, my heart didn't.

Jimin, weren't you cold going around in these clothes? I couldn't buy you one nice coat when I knew you were sensitive to cold. I'm told you're in the mountains. I think it must be awfully windy there. Are you dressed warmly enough? I think of you even more come winter, you know. Granny's real worried you might be shivering in clothes like these.

You were one curious child, weren't ya. Grandma! You'd call me and say the funniest things. Do ants sleep under blankies like I do? Who switches the sky on and off to bring morning and night? Granny marveled where you'd come from with your funny words. I'd lived for over four decades without knowing you—where were you in all that time? Where'd you come from to tell me these marvelous things?

You remember when I was hospitalized because I came down with the flu? Why, you came to see me by yourself after school carrying your backpack. You had grass stains on the knees of your P.E. uniform pants. When I said, What on earth are you doing here?, you gave me what you had in your hands. Three four-leaf clovers. You placed them on my palms and said, Grandma, please don't die or get sick, either. Granny laughed because you were so cute, but your eyes were full of tears. Jimin, it's strange, but thinking about that moment still breaks my heart. Why search till you get grass stains on your pants for little old me? Why fill your eyes with tears for little old me? My cutie patootie, my baby.

Her writing grew less legible as her hands lost strength, yet Malja didn't stop writing the letter. Jimin would be able to read her writing no matter how terrible it was.

Malja folded the letter she would give Jimin in person, at the place no mail carrier could access, the place no letter could reach, and hugged it to her heart.

Translator's Note

On April 16, 2014, the MV *Sewol* sank off the coast of South Korea, claiming the lives of 304 passengers, most of them high school students on a school trip to Jeju Island. Two probationary (contract) teachers, Kim Cho-won and Lee Ji-hye, died while trying to save their students. But as probationary teachers are not considered public servants under Korean law, Kim's and Lee's deaths, unlike those of their tenured colleagues, were not acknowledged as line-of-duty, disentitling their families to death benefits. After three years of petitions by their families, their deaths were recognized as line-of-duty by a presidential order on Teachers' Day. To this day, the facts surrounding the sinking have not been fully investigated, and the bereaved families still demand answers.

Author's Note

The summer I was thirty, I remember standing in the Korean fiction section of Bandi & Luni's in Jongno—how I stood rooted to the spot for a long time, wondering, *Was I never going to make it?* A life of writing and publishing books was far out of my reach, and slipping further away yet. I had submitted stories to many contests over two years but had not received a single honorable mention, let alone win. "Shoko's Smile," which I had worked hard on that spring, was also eliminated in the first round of a contest.

I was at the end of my rope. I didn't have a proper job, I certainly was paying off loans every month, and I was under constant financial strain. Under such conditions, I felt it would be impossible to continue on my hopeless mission. Despite wanting to write and publish and live as a writer, I thought the time had finally come to give up. Reflecting on the prospect by myself, I cried my eyes out. I cried like a person deciding to let go of someone they loved for a long time.

Whenever I become lax or lazy with my writing, I recall my state of mind when those tears were shed. This was the only thing I ever truly wanted to do in life. I don't know if it was a delusion or fantasy, but I wanted to live as someone who wrote.

After making my literary debut, I wrote with the feelings of someone dating a longtime crush. The completion of a sentence, a paragraph, a story was in itself a joy. The long, slow hours of sitting at my desk, only to write a few lines, were precisely what made me come alive. Some wounds could only be healed when I was absorbed in writing.

I was too harsh on myself during my teens and twenties. I would like to apologize to the old me for hating and unfairly treating myself just because I was who I was. I'd like to cook a delicious meal for that girl, massage her shoulders, and tell her everything will be alright. I'd like to take her to a warm, bright place and listen to her story. And thank her for gathering her courage, even though she is such a coward, and accompanying me to this point.

I think this is the only present I can give my dad, who recently retired. I am glad the book is a joy to my mom, too. I salute my baby brother, who is holding his own in the daily grind. My deepest gratitude to my maternal grandma and grandpa, who went through a lot of trouble to raise the eccentric, sensitive child that I was. I received enough love from them to last me a lifetime and more. I am also grateful to my dear aunt and uncle. Thank you to my cats, Leo, Mio, Mari, and Potter.

I want to thank my friends who are always by my side in spirit. I don't know how to express my gratitude to Jihye Unni, who steadied me and supported me when I was reeling. Thank you to critic Seo Yeongchae, writer Kim Yeonsu, and the editors at Munhakdongne.

I'd like to thank everyone who gave me an opportunity, who believed in a totally unverified, unestablished writer. I will not forget the precious trust you have placed in me and hope to be a writer who produces good writing for years to come. I hope to be a writer who views people and the world from the side of those who are scorned and hated for the sole reason of being themselves. I hope that on that path, I too can be fearlessly and utterly myself.

Summer 2016
Choi Eunyoung